Her Kind of Cowboy

Center Point
Large Print

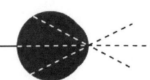

**This Large Print Book carries the
Seal of Approval of N.A.V.H.**

Her Kind of Cowboy

Charlotte Douglas

CENTER POINT LARGE PRINT
THORNDIKE, MAINE

This Center Point Large Print edition
is published in the year 2014 by arrangement with
Harlequin Books S.A.

The text of this Large Print edition is unabridged.
In other aspects, this book may vary
from the original edition.
Printed in the United States of America
on permanent paper.
Set in 16-point Times New Roman type.

ISBN: 978-1-62899-260-1

Library of Congress Cataloging-in-Publication Data

Douglas, Charlotte.
 Her kind of cowboy / Charlotte Douglas. — Center Point Large Print
edition.
  pages ; cm
  Summary: "Caroline Tuttle dreams of moving out West and marrying a
cowboy; but when a friend wills Caroline a farm and leaves her with
two final wishes—to care for an orphaned girl and the farm's tenant,
plans change"—Provided by publisher.
  ISBN 978-1-62899-260-1 (library binding : alk. paper)
  1. Cowboys—Fiction. 2. Large type books. I. Title.
 PS3604.O9254H47 2014
 813′.6—dc23
                                                           2014026318

Her Kind of
Cowboy

Chapter One

"Have you finished everything on your list?" Agnes Tuttle asked.

Glancing up from the kitchen island countertop she was scrubbing, Caroline eyed her mother with a mixture of affection and exasperation. Caroline loved her only parent, without doubt, but Agnes's expectations sometimes suffocated her.

Today was one of those days.

Agnes, a soft, plump woman in her late fifties with hair artificially colored the hue of ripe apricots, hovered in the hall doorway, ready to take flight. She wore her best summer dress and patent leather pumps and a matching purse draped over her arm, all in the same subdued orange shade as her tight curls and the bright swaths of rouge on her cheeks.

Caroline pushed a strand of blond hair off her forehead and straightened, easing the muscles in her back. "I've scrubbed the bathrooms, changed the linens in all six bedrooms, dusted and vacuumed. And I'm almost through with the kitchen. I still have to do the laundry and run errands."

Sheesh, sometimes she felt like Cinderella. Except there were no pesky stepsisters, no upcoming ball and no Prince Charming waiting in the wings. No nasty stepmother, either. Just a mother who loved her and had relied on her totally for too many years.

"Don't put the sheets in the dryer," Agnes said, as she invariably did. "Hang them on the line. I want them to smell like sunshine and fresh air."

"Yes, ma'am."

It did no good to argue that by Friday, when the next wave of weekend guests arrived at the Tuttle Bed and Breakfast in Pleasant Valley, South Carolina, the linens' scent of sunshine would have long since dissipated. Her mother had always had her standards, although Caroline often wondered if Agnes had to do the work herself to live up to them whether her requirements would have remained as stringent.

"I'll be at Aunt Mona's until tomorrow," Agnes reminded her.

Caroline nodded. Every Monday, her mother made the trek to Walhalla, less than an hour away by car, to spend the day with her sister. Because Agnes didn't drive after dark, she stayed overnight. Caroline welcomed the regular respites. Agnes, who claimed to suffer from a long list of ailments that none of the doctors at the medical center had been able to confirm or cure, depended on Caroline, her only child, to keep the massive old Victorian house in immaculate condition for their guests. Only when Agnes left town did Caroline feel that her life was her own.

"Have a good time, Mama, and kiss Aunt Mona for me." She held her breath, praying her mother would leave before thinking of more items to add to the to-do list.

A few hours later, reveling in her brief freedom, Caroline lay on the thick grass of the lawn of the deep backyard, folded her arms behind her head and followed the progress of a single wispy cloud across the brilliant blue sky. The heady fragrance of roses, the thick sweetness of honeysuckle, and the pungency of recently mowed grass, distinctive smells of summer, filled her nostrils and lifted her spirits. The late June sun warmed her like a blessing. Only the drone of bumblebees, lumbering through the Queen Anne's lace and black-eyed Susans in the meadow beyond the back fence, and the snap of freshly laundered sheets on the clothesline behind the garage broke the drowsy silence.

Caroline had been at work since before sunup, preparing breakfast for departing weekend guests. After the meal, she'd finished the cleaning and prepared the week's shopping list. Errands to Paulie's Drug Store to refill her mother's numerous prescriptions and to Blalock's to buy groceries had taken most of the afternoon. Now, except for retrieving the sun-dried linens from the lines and folding them away, Caroline was finished with work for the day. The B and B had no reservations for the night, and she was contentedly free to do anything she wanted, or nothing, if she pleased.

"You're thirty-three and need a life of your own, Caroline," her friend Eileen Bickerstaff had told her for the umpteenth time last week as they'd enjoyed a cup of tea at Eileen's kitchen table at Blackberry Farm, ten miles out of town at the west end of Pleasant Valley. "Your mother's perfectly capable of taking care of herself. And she can hire a girl from town for the housework she has you doing. Maria Ortega's younger sister Rosa would be happy for the job."

At ninety-eight, decades older than Agnes Tuttle, Eileen had managed quite well by herself for more than sixty years, with only occasional help the last few years from Caroline with the heavy cleaning. The spry, elderly woman could literally run circles around Agnes with her hypochondria and self-professed weak heart.

"I'll have a life of my own soon," Caroline had assured Eileen. "You know I've been saving my pay from both you and Mother for years. When I have enough, I'll make my move."

Now, basking in the sun, Caroline felt a smile of satisfaction tugging at her lips. In another year, she'd have the nest egg she needed. She loved her mother and she loved Pleasant Valley, but she loved the prospect of freedom and being responsible to no one but herself more. Next year, with her savings in hand, she'd tell her mother and friends goodbye and head west. Maybe to Colorado or Montana. Or more likely Texas, New Mexico or Arizona, where she'd find a temporary job until she could locate a small piece of land she could afford, buy horses and a few cattle, and live out her dreams.

She closed her eyes and pictured the scene. Wide-open spaces, rugged mesas, high chaparral and lonesome piñon pines. Quaint little towns with a single main street lined with stores with wooden facades, plank sidewalks and hitching posts out front.

And cowboys.

She sighed at the prospect. She'd always loved cowboys.

Her dreams hadn't really changed in the fifteen years since she'd graduated from Pleasant Valley High. They'd only become more focused. In college, she had pursued a business degree and hoped to use those skills to escape the valley where she'd lived all her life. But her father's untimely death had ended her college career during her junior year. Wallace Tuttle had left an insurance policy, but it wasn't enough to pay college tuition or even to support Agnes through her remaining years. With Caroline's encouragement, Agnes had turned the enormous family home into a thriving bed-and-breakfast. At the time, Caroline had volunteered to help.

She hadn't intended that offer to become a life sentence.

Only her goal of moving out west and having her own place had sustained her through the years of her mother's unceasing demands and bouts of so-called illness. To avoid the harsh reality of her mother's complaints and bossiness while she planned and saved for her move, Caroline had escaped into fantasy. Immersing herself in Western culture, she'd devoured Louis L'Amour and Zane Grey novels and watched classic movies like *Silverado*, *Lonesome Dove* and Clint Eastwood's spaghetti westerns until she could quote the dialogue by heart. The books and movies had whetted her appetite for all things cowboy.

Her eyelids drooped against the bright sunlight. Soon, she assured herself, she'd shake the dust of the valley from her feet. Even if escalating real estate values meant she had to take a temporary job out west before she could afford her own place, she would make her break by next year or find herself smothered by Agnes's expectations and tethered to her mother's apron strings forever.

Soon, she promised herself.

She sighed, nestled deeper into the soft grass, and closed her eyes.

A keening wind howled down the deserted main street, scattering tumbleweeds and spawning wind devils that spewed dust in their paths. The relentless sun beat down with thin warmth, casting the tall shadow of a lone figure in the middle of the street, six-guns strapped to his hips, determined eyes vigilant beneath the shadow of his Stetson. The only hope for the frightened citizens against the outlaws who terrorized them, the lawman lifted his steely gaze toward the edge of town, where riders approached in a thunder of hooves and a swirl of dust. Without taking his eyes from the oncoming desperadoes, he called to the people cowering behind closed doors.

"Hello?" the deep voice said.

Caroline's eyes flew open, but she had to be dreaming still. The tall man with broad shoulders stood between her and the sun, so that all she could see was his silhouette. The town was safe. At well over six feet with an imposing build, he was a bulwark against all outlaws. His hands rested on the butts of his six-guns, ready for action.

"I knocked on the front door." His voice, while rich and pleasing, held no distinctive Western twang. "When no one answered, I came around back. I need a room for the next few nights. Do you have a vacancy?"

His words finally registered in her sleep-numbed brain, and Caroline came fully awake and leaped to her feet.

The man's hands weren't resting on six-guns, but tucked in the back pockets of his jeans. She shifted to see his face in the sunlight, and his resemblance to the perfectly handsome Western hero of her dreams faded, although the stranger's chiseled features would have looked terrific beneath a broad-brimmed cowboy hat. Dressed in jeans, work boots and a faded navy T-shirt, he wasn't handsome in the classic sense, but his rugged looks were very easy on the eyes. His hazel irises, deep brown flecked with grass-green, reflected both tranquility and an underlying pain, and his tanned face crinkled in an engaging smile that exposed perfect white teeth. She guessed he was in his early thirties, close to her age.

"Sorry if I woke you," he said.

"I was only daydreaming." Caroline, suddenly conscious of her tousled hair, grass-stained shorts and rumpled shirt, combed her fingers through her hair and tugged at her blouse in a futile attempt to straighten it. "You said you need a room?"

He nodded, hands still tucked in his pockets as if he were hiding them. "If you have one."

His warm grin was contagious, and she returned it with a smile of her own. "I have six. You can take your pick. Follow me."

Rather than take a guest through the back door, she circled the house, navigating the brick walkway through the wisteria arbor, draped with fragrant lavender blooms. The stranger's gaze burned between her shoulder blades, and she chided herself for noticing. Even though he was the best-looking man to hit the valley since attorney Randall Benedict's arrival from New York last year, he remained a stranger, merely passing through. With plans for her move west still buzzing in her brain, she needed a man like a fish needed a bicycle, no matter how appealing he appeared, so his good looks were a moot point.

She entered the foyer, its coolness a welcome contrast to the summer heat. In a corner beneath the massive staircase with its polished newel post, a small writing desk held the guest registration book. She handed the stranger a pen. "I'll need your name, home address, and car license tag number."

When he reached for the pen, she stifled a sympathetic cry. Scar tissue, raised welts of pale skin, covered the backs of his large, powerful hands that looked as if they'd been horribly burned. She turned quickly to the board behind her to grab a room key and hoped he hadn't noticed her reaction.

"Headed for the mountains?" she asked in a neutral voice.

Most of the visitors at Tuttle's B and B considered Pleasant Valley a way station on their trips to the Great Smoky Mountains National Park in western North Carolina and eastern Tennessee. A few, however, came to fly-fish in the rapids of the Piedmont River that bisected the valley. And, occasionally, business travelers stayed overnight. But this man didn't seem to fit any of those categories.

He signed the guest book in bold, flowing strokes with only a slight hesitation in the movements of his damaged hand. "I'm moving to a new home."

She lifted her eyebrows. "Here in town?"

Still concentrating on his registration, he shook his head. "I'm stopping off here so I don't arrive at my new place ahead of my furniture."

He finished his entry, and she swiveled the book to read what he'd written.

Ethan Garrison. Baltimore, Maryland.

So he was headed to Maryland, a full day of driving from Pleasant Valley. Headed east, not west. Too bad. He had the build and, from what little she'd observed, the quiet, stoic temperament of a cowboy. But instead of wrangling cattle, he'd probably be working in some stuffy office in the city of Baltimore, where his deep tan would soon fade. Even a boring business suit, however, wouldn't dim his killer smile.

With a mental shake, she reminded herself that the man might be married, although his scarred left hand bore no gold band. She handed him a key.

"Your room's at the top of the stairs on the left. Our best view. Overlooks the valley and the mountains in the distance. It has an adjoining bath. And if it's not to your liking, I can show you others."

"I'm sure it will be fine." His expression was friendly, but a residual sadness flickered in his eyes. "Okay if I leave my truck out front?"

"Sure. Or you can park it in the lot on the east side of the house. Your choice."

"Thanks." His gaze held hers for a beat, as if he wanted to say more but didn't. He pivoted and headed for the entrance.

The screen door slammed behind him, and Caroline took the stairs two at a time to the third floor and raced to her room at the back of the house to change clothes and comb her hair. With an unexpected guest, she had more shopping to do and hoped that Jodie was still open.

Ethan sauntered down the front walk of the B and B toward his pickup, parked at the curb. He paused, inhaled a deep breath of the summer air and with it the faint aroma of smoke. At the scent, his chest constricted, and in a rush of panic, he struggled to breathe. Sweat beaded his brow, and he clenched his hands to stop their trembling.

Just someone burning brush nearby, he assured himself, but only several minutes of deep breathing and regimented self-control enabled him to slow his galloping pulse and relax the all-too-familiar tightness in his chest. The scars on the back of his hands itched with an intensity almost as painful as his initial injuries.

Concentrate on something else, anything else.

He refused to experience an emotional melt-down, especially not on the quiet street of a strange town. He focused on the giant maples, thick with summer foliage, whose arched branches shaded the broad avenue from the summer heat. The neighborhood, with its century-old homes on oversize lots and surrounded by colorful beds of flowers, was a throwback to a different time, a perfect setting for *The Andy Griffith Show*. Ethan half expected to see a barefooted Opie come whistling down the street with a fishing pole slung over his shoulder.

The image, conjured from television reruns he'd watched during his recuperation, calmed him. With his panic conquered, at least for the moment, he recalled another pleasant image. The pretty woman he'd found sprawled asleep in the grass behind the bed-and-breakfast had been a delightful surprise. He should have awakened her imme-diately. Instead, he'd taken a moment to appreciate the gracefulness of her bare arms, her short, thick hair the color of sunshine, and her cheeks flushed as pink as the roses that rambled along the split rail fence at the back of the yard. Best of all, however, had been the startling cornflower blue of her wide eyes when she'd awakened, a hue as deep and magnificent as the Carolina sky. His admiration of the woman gave him hope.

Ethan, old buddy, maybe you're not dried-up and dead inside after all.

His panic defeated and his outlook more

optimistic than it had been in months, he whistled a Montgomery Gentry tune, climbed into his pickup, started the engine, and backed his truck into the parking lot. He doubted the crime rate was high in this small Southern town, but he didn't want to risk his belongings, securely stowed under a tarp in the bed of his truck, by leaving them on the street, ripe for picking.

After positioning his truck in the space directly beneath the security light, he shut off the engine, grabbed his duffel bag from the passenger seat, climbed out and keyed the lock.

On the front porch, a screen door slammed. The pretty woman—hell, maybe he *was* dead, or at least his brain, he hadn't even asked her name— scampered down the wide front stairs, hurried down the front walk and took the sidewalk that led to the town's main street. She'd changed into a floral dress that caught his attention, showing off her nice figure.

Don't get carried away. She's probably married and runs this place with her husband.

Disappointment engulfed him at the thought, because he couldn't get over the impression he'd had from the first time he saw her that this woman was someone he'd been waiting for, for a long, long time.

He hoisted his bag to his shoulder and headed for the entrance. He'd be at the B and B a few more days. Plenty of time to learn her name.

• • •

Caroline cut through the alley between Jay-Jay's Garage and Fulton's Department Store and hurried across Piedmont Avenue, the town's main street, to Jodie's Mountain Crafts and Café. It was past the café's four o'clock closing time, but Caroline was counting on Jodie's still being there to let her in. Otherwise, she'd have to return home and do her own baking for her guest's breakfast tomorrow.

The "closed" sign hung in plain view inside the double front doors, but when Caroline pressed her face to the glass, she spotted Jodie Davidson, the owner, sitting at the counter beside the cash register and figuring up the day's receipts. Caroline rapped on the glass with her knuckles. Jodie looked up, spotted her and smiled. In less than a minute, she had the door open and was motioning Caroline to a seat at the counter.

"How 'bout a glass of iced tea?" Jodie asked. "I was just about to pour myself one."

"Sounds good."

Caroline had known Jodie all her life, and, with her brown, sun-streaked hair, cheerleader-fresh face, and trim figure, the café's owner looked remarkably like the teenager Caroline remembered. But her friendship with Jodie went back even further than their teen years to the days when Jodie had bird-dogged the steps of her older brother Grant, whom she adored. Jodie had slipped away from her mother's watchful eye one bright fall morning and appeared at the door of Caroline's second-grade classroom. Grant had been more worried about his little sister than embarrassed, causing Caroline to develop a crush on the boy that had lasted through high school. Now Grant was married to Merrilee Stratton and they had a child of their own. All her friends had moved on with their lives. Only Caroline was stuck in a Pleasant Valley limbo.

In a series of deft moves, Jodie scooped crushed ice into two glasses, filled them with sweet tea, garnished the rims with lemon wedges, and set them on the counter.

"I don't know how you do it," Caroline said.

Jodie laughed. "I've been working this counter so many years, I could serve beverages in my sleep."

Caroline took a sip and shook her head. "I'm not talking about just the café. You run this business, raise Brittany, and help Jeff ride herd on the boys at Archer Farm. Don't you ever get tired?"

The entire town had been abuzz when Jeff Davidson, the resident bad boy, had returned to Pleasant Valley after a hitch in the military. With four other former Marines, he'd opened his facility for at-risk teenage boys. Not only had Archer Farm proved a success, Jeff had married Jodie and adopted her teenage daughter.

"I doubt I work half as hard as you," Jodie said. "How's your mother?"

"In Walhalla with Aunt Mona. And I have an unexpected guest. Please tell me you have muffins so I don't have to go home and bake."

"Cranberry-pecan, apple cinnamon, or blueberry-walnut?"

"All of the above. If this guy's size is any indicator, I'm guessing his appetite is huge."

"Businessman?" Jodie asked.

Caroline shrugged. "Don't know. He's just passing through on a move to Baltimore."

"You okay there by yourself?" Concern shone in Jodie's hazel eyes.

"There's a dead bolt on the door to our private rooms. I'm as safe as anyone is these days. And the police department is only a block away." She rolled her eyes. "And nosy neighbors even closer."

Jodie opened the door of a stainless steel freezer, removed three packages of frozen muffins, dropped them into a plastic bag, and placed it on the counter. "I don't know why you buy these from me. Your baking's better than mine."

"Thanks, but yours take the prize. Besides, I have so little time to myself, I hate to spend it in the kitchen."

The bell on the front door jingled, indicating a new arrival. A tall, good-looking man with dark brown hair and matching eyes closed the door behind him.

"Hi, Rand," Jodie greeted the newcomer. "What's up?"

Randall Benedict rented the office suite over Jodie's café for his law practice. Last October, he'd married Brynn Sawyer, another of Caroline's lifelong friends, and had made a permanent move from New York to the valley.

"Hi, Jodie. Caroline, I'm glad you're here. I stopped by your house, but your guest said you'd gone to town."

Rand's eyes were troubled, and thin-set lips and a tightened jaw replaced his usual rakish grin.

"Is something wrong?" Caroline's heart stuttered. Why would the attorney seek her out? Had her mother had an accident and he'd been drafted to break the bad news? "Is it Mama?"

"As far as I know, your mother's fine," Rand assured her quickly, "but I have some sad news."

The skin on the back of her neck tingled, and, in a flash of precognition, Caroline took a deep breath and waited, knowing that what Rand was about to say would change her life forever.

"It's Eileen Bickerstaff at Blackberry Farm," he said. "She died last night."

Chapter Two

In Rand's law office above the café, Caroline fidgeted in the maroon leather chair beside his mahogany desk. The cold from the plastic bag of frozen muffins in her lap seeped through the thin fabric of her dress and chilled her thighs. She shivered with cold and grief. Eileen, despite her age, had seemed healthy and vibrant. Her death came as a shock.

"I don't understand," Caroline said. "What's so urgent that you have to tell me now?"

Rand reached into the top right drawer, withdrew an envelope and slid it across the desk. "Before you open that, there's something you need to know."

"Poor Eileen." Tears prickled the back of her eyelids. The elderly woman had been more than an employer. She'd been a friend and confidante, a source of unconditional acceptance and affection, more loving and maternal than her own mother. Caroline had known that Eileen was ninety-eight, but the old woman had seemed timeless, and Caroline had expected her friend to be around as long as Caroline remained in the valley. She'd never considered the possibility that Eileen would die before Caroline made her break.

"I know this is hard for you," Rand said. "We're

all shocked by Eileen's death. Especially Brynn. She's the one who found her."

Brynn had resigned as an officer with the police department when she'd married Rand last year and moved to River Walk, the house on Valley Road nearest Blackberry Farm.

"If it's any consolation," Rand was saying, "Eileen's passing was peaceful. She died in her sleep with a smile on her face."

Caroline glanced at the envelope where her name was scrawled in Eileen's elegant but spidery script. "What is it I need to know?"

"Eileen left you a bequest."

Caroline swallowed hard to keep from sobbing. Dear Eileen. She'd probably provided a small contribution to what she'd dubbed Caroline's Escape Plan.

Rand's next words took Caroline's breath away. "She left you Blackberry Farm and all her savings."

"What?" Caroline reeled with shock. Rand had to be mistaken. "That's not possible."

"I drew up the will myself last year, remember? You were there."

"But I didn't know its contents. I only witnessed her signature. Why would she leave everything to me?"

"Eileen told me you were like the daughter she never had. She had no living relatives, and she knew you would appreciate Blackberry Farm with its long history in the valley."

Guilt stung Caroline as deeply as grief. As the reality of Eileen's bequest had sunk in, her first thought had been to sell the property. The thousand-acre farm, complete with two houses in addition to the main farmhouse, would bring more than enough money to finance Caroline's move west and buy the ranch she'd always wanted. Eileen, however, had apparently left her the place with the hope that Caroline would remain in the valley. But her friend's expectation didn't make sense. Eileen, more than anyone, had known Caroline's dreams of owning a ranch out west, far away from Pleasant Valley.

"Are there conditions to the bequest?" she asked.

Rand hesitated. "Not exactly."

"Not exactly what?"

"The property and bank account are yours, free and clear. But there's the letter Eileen left you. She must have sensed she was dying, because it's dated yesterday. She left me a copy."

Caroline's gaze fell on the envelope again.

"Read it," Rand said. "It explains everything."

With trembling fingers and conflicting emotions, Caroline opened the envelope and withdrew the letter that Eileen must have produced on the printer that sat beside her well-used computer on her living room desk.

My dear Caroline,

If you are reading this, it means that I am gone. Don't cry for me, child. I've had a long and interesting life, and your delightful friendship was one of its high points. I'm happy to leave Blackberry Farm to you. Yes, I know you're itching to escape the valley, and eventually, if you wish to sell the property and head west, I've no objections. But before you go, I have two favors to ask.

I hadn't expected to make my exit so soon and have other plans in the works that I need you to carry out for me. First is Hannah, Daniel's little sister.

Caroline glanced from the page to Rand. "Daniel? At Archer Farm?"

The likable teenage boy had been the greatest success of Jeff Davidson's social experiment. A good kid who'd fallen in with the wrong crowd, Daniel had blossomed under the care and guidance of Jeff's Marines. He'd become a responsible worker in Jodie's café, made the Dean's List at Pleasant Valley High and turned his life around. With his juvenile record sealed by the courts, Daniel was well on his way to becoming a productive citizen.

"Daniel came from a single-parent home," Rand said. "His mother's recent death left his nine-year-old sister alone."

With dread settling like bricks in the pit of her stomach, Caroline turned back to Eileen's letter.

Rand has made all the arrangements for me to serve as foster mother to nine-year-old Hannah, so she can be near her brother, her only living relative. Hannah is scheduled to arrive next week. You are under no legal obligation—and Blackberry Farm will be yours, regardless—but I'm asking as a favor that you take over guardianship of Hannah, at least until Daniel graduates from high school next year. I'm certain Rand can take care of the legal technicalities.

Caroline eyed Rand with dismay. "I don't know anything about children!"

"Believe me, I can relate," Rand said with a wry smile. He'd taken custody of his two-year-old nephew last year after the death of Jared's parents in a car crash. "You have to keep in mind that all first-time parents are new to the experience. It's a learn-as-you-go proposition."

Stunned by Eileen's first request, Caroline was almost afraid to read the second.

If the prospect of Hannah hasn't scared you off, my second request might seem easier. I want you to honor the year-long lease I signed recently for Orchard Cottage.

Orchard Cottage, Caroline recalled, was the small house at the edge of Blackberry Farm's apple orchards. Included in the complex were an ancient barn and numerous outbuildings.

> I've rented the place to an artist who wants the barn for his studio. He will arrive in a few days. He's counting on this, and I'm hoping you won't disappoint him. His payments will provide you some extra income.

"A tenant," Caroline said with relief. "That's not a problem." Especially compared to a resident nine-year-old.

Rand lifted his eyebrows. "Keep reading."

Leery of what she'd find, Caroline returned to Eileen's letter.

> As part of the lease agreement, I have promised to provide lunch and dinner daily to the tenant. I had originally figured the arrangement would provide company for me and free his time for his artwork. I hope you can honor this facet of the lease.

Caroline stifled a groan. A guest for lunch and dinner every day? She might as well be running her own bed-and-breakfast. Then she gave herself a mental shake. How could she not honor Eileen's wishes after the woman's incredible generosity in leaving her Blackberry Farm? An ironic twist of fate had left her with both the means to make her immediate escape from the valley and obligations that would keep her here another year.

"Well?" Rand had been studying her face. "What do you think?"

"I'm still in shock." She quickly read the remaining lines of the letter and choked back tears at the warm words of affection. "I'll need to think about Eileen's requests and let you know."

Rand followed her to the door. "I'm sure you'll do the right thing."

"Will you notify me about the funeral arrangements?"

"You'll be first on my list."

Caroline thanked him and hurried down the stairs. Easy for Rand to say she'd do the right thing. She was the one who had to figure out what the right thing was.

Ethan sprawled on the porch steps of the old Victorian, his elbows on the stair tread behind him, his feet crossed at the ankles on the bottom step. Contentment, an alien emotion, settled over him, eased his breathing and slowed his pulse. For the first time since making his decision to move from the city where he'd spent his entire life, he felt at peace with his choice. He missed his parents and sister, but he couldn't endure another Sunday supper with Jerry's chair empty, his place setting forever removed. The vacant space chided

Ethan louder than any words of blame. The absence of his brother's grinning mug across the table had been a painful reminder of Ethan's inadequacy, his failure to be there when Jerry had needed him most.

His family swore they didn't fault Ethan, but the agony in his mother's face, the perpetual slump of his father's strong shoulders and the missing sparkle in his sister Amber's eyes seared deeper than any words of blame. He hoped his move would grant him the serenity to come to terms with the past. If his current state of mind was any indicator, he was on the right track.

Although the temperature had soared earlier in the day, deep shade from an ancient magnolia held the late afternoon heat at bay and cooled the porch. Above the hum of a central air-conditioning unit next door floated the notes from a piano, a classical piece that soared and swirled. He appreciated the beauty of the strange music and welcomed the fact that its unfamiliar tune triggered no memories. He'd learned through experience that he couldn't escape them, not with alcohol nor medication. Exhaustive physical labor often helped, but not always. He'd also learned that he could handle memories better when they didn't ambush him, triggered by a sound, a scent, a sight or a few key words.

Post-traumatic stress disorder, his therapist had called it, and warned Ethan that running away wouldn't stop the cascade of terrifying flash-backs and painful memories, either. But Ethan had to try.

There will be peace in the valley for me some day.

The line from his mother's favorite gospel hymn popped into his head. Maybe the haunting melody was an omen, he prayed. He'd been through hell the last few months. He could use some peace.

Footsteps on the walk scattered his thoughts. The owner of the bed-and-breakfast had returned, her golden hair glistening in the sunlight. She was carrying a plastic bag with a Jodie's Mountain Crafts and Café logo and looking as if she'd seen a ghost.

He rose to his feet to meet her. "You okay?"

She'd been walking with her head down. At his question, she jerked her chin up and gazed at him. Her enticing blue eyes widened with a mixture of confusion and surprise, as if she'd never seen him before.

"Ethan Garrison," he reminded her. "I checked in earlier."

"Of course." A flush as pink as summer roses brought the color back to her cheeks.

"You didn't tell me your name."

"I'm Caroline Tuttle." She sounded distracted, making him wonder what had happened in the short time she'd been gone that had shaken her former poise.

Something about the woman stirred his protective instincts. "You sure you're all right?"

She nodded and moved around him to climb the stairs.

"Wait, please." He cast about for something to say, anything to keep her with him a little while longer.

"Yes?" A tiny line between her feathery eyebrows marred the porcelain perfection of her forehead, and he felt himself going under for the third time in the shimmering depths of her deep blue eyes.

Then he noted the bag in her hand and found a way to keep the conversation rolling. "Is this Jodie's Café open for dinner?"

She shook her head, and the scent of her shampoo, evocative of the wisteria covering the side arbor, filled his nostrils. "Jodie's place is open only for breakfast and lunch."

"Is there somewhere I can grab a bite?" He wasn't really interested in food, but the topic gave him a good excuse to keep talking.

"The closest restaurant is Ridge's Barbecue, but it's twelve miles east on the main highway."

He sighed. "I've been driving since before dawn. The last thing I want now is to climb back behind the wheel. I guess I'll make do with the crackers and Coke left in the cooler in my truck."

"Or you could have supper here with me."

He searched her face for signs of flirtation, but

found only Southern hospitality. But he would take what he could get. He couldn't remember the last time he'd shared a meal with a beautiful woman. Or had wanted to this badly. "I don't want to impose on you and your family."

"Mama's visiting her sister, so it's just me for supper. If you'll join me, I won't have to eat alone."

This was his lucky day. "You're sure it's no trouble?"

"Not a bit."

Okay, so she'd lied. But the trouble wasn't in preparing supper. The trouble was the six-foot-plus of gorgeous man sitting at the island in her kitchen. Caroline had wanted something to distract her from the sadness of Eileen's death, but she should have been more careful what she'd wished for. Any more distraction and she'd be chopping off her fingers instead of slicing tomatoes.

"Sure you don't want some help?" Ethan propped his elbows on the island. "I've done a lot of cooking in my line of work."

"Are you a chef?" Somehow she couldn't picture him in a chef's apron and hat. A business suit didn't fit, either. With his short-cropped brown hair and intense gaze, he reminded her of the actor Chritian Bale, a man capable of saving the world—or at least his little corner of it.

"Not a chef. A firefighter."

"Ah." So she hadn't been far off in her analysis. And firefighting explained the horrible burns on the back of his hands. But he didn't seem the type who wanted sympathy, so she kept her tone light. "One of those guys who runs into the buildings everyone else is running out of."

"It's mostly sitting around twiddling my thumbs and waiting for a call." The warmth of his smile was at least four-alarm. "Unless it's my rotation for kitchen duty."

What was it about this man that had her stomach doing a happy dance? She focused her attention on scooping seeds from a cantaloupe, and the explanation hit her. She'd grown up with every male close to her age in the valley—not counting Rand Benedict. All of them were now married and settled down, except for Lucas Rhodes, an officer with the police department. So Ethan Garrison was the first unattached male she'd met in a long, long time whom she didn't regard as a brother.

Or *was* he unattached?

She arranged wedges of melon and tomato, along with slices of country ham, on a white stoneware platter. "Moving across country must be a chore."

"And an adventure," he added.

Well, why not, she might as well fish for information. "Will your family be joining you?"

Agony flickered across his face, and she wished she could call the question back.

"I'm traveling solo." His neutral tone seemed tightly controlled.

She hastened to change the subject in hopes of easing his discomfort. "I'll be moving across country soon myself."

"You're selling the bed-and-breakfast?" He lifted his eyebrows in surprise.

"It belongs to my mother. She'll keep it open after I'm gone."

She'd said those words recently to Eileen. And now Eileen, one of her dearest friends on Earth, was gone. Out of the blue, the full impact of Eileen's death hit her like a runaway eighteen-wheeler, and a sob escaped before she could hold it back.

In a flash, she found herself wrapped in Ethan's strong arms, her face pressed against his chest, her tears staining his T-shirt. He smelled of sunshine and leather. Holding her with unexpected gentleness for such a big man, he didn't try to stop her crying.

"Let it all out," he murmured against her hair. "Whatever it is, you'll feel better for it."

Her loss of control in front of a perfect stranger—perfect in every way—horrified her. His strong arms were both consoling and unsettling. Forcing herself to abandon the comforting warmth, Caroline pushed away, crossed the kitchen and plucked tissues from a box of Kleenex.

"Sorry." She wiped her eyes and blew her nose. "I just found out that a friend of mine passed away last night."

The pain returned to his eyes, and he nodded with understanding. "It's hard losing a friend."

"She was quite old. She'd lived a good life and it was her time. I thought those facts would make her passing easier, but they don't."

"Look, you're dealing with a loss," he said with appealing gentleness. "I can grab a snack from my cooler. You don't have to feed me, especially under the circumstances."

"No! Please stay." She shuddered at the need in her voice and tossed the crumpled tissues into the trash. "I don't want to be alone right now."

"You're sure?"

Between Eileen's unexpected death and Ethan's provocative presence, Caroline was more befuddled than sure, but she nodded. "There's wine in the fridge. Would you like a glass?"

"Okay. Thanks."

She retrieved the bottle of white wine from the refrigerator. Ethan took it and the corkscrew from her, and she removed long-stemmed glasses from the cupboard. With a deft twist, Ethan popped the cork and filled the glasses. He handed her one, and their fingers touched, sending a frisson of delight up her arm.

What was happening to her? Was Eileen's death

making her crazy? She took a deep breath to steady her whirling senses.

Ethan lifted his glass in a toast. Their gazes locked, and compassion glimmered in the green brilliance of his hazel eyes.

"To absent friends." His deep voice was thick with emotion.

She raised her glass, but discovered she had to clear her throat before she could speak. "To absent friends."

They both drank, and Ethan settled once more on the stool beside the island. "Now, how about telling me all about this town you'll be leaving soon?"

Chapter Three

"That was a great meal," Ethan said later. "I appreciate your taking the trouble."

"You're welcome, but it wasn't any trouble." Caroline was determined to remain quiet. She'd done far too much talking during supper, encouraged by Ethan's questions about the town. She'd left him little time to tell her about himself, and she was curious about the handsome stranger with the badly burned hands.

They were sitting on the screened back porch in wicker rockers, watching lightning bugs flit through the deep shadows of the garden. Jasmine and honeysuckle scented the air. The rising full moon cast silvery dapples on the lawn and added another element of romance to the night.

If she was thinking of romance, Eileen's death had definitely sent her off the deep end. Sure, Ethan Garrison was drop-dead gorgeous. Also kind, gentle, amusing, probably even a hometown hero, but he was also only passing through, and she had more important issues to occupy her mind. She had yet to decide whether to remain in the valley to honor Eileen's requests about Hannah, the foster child, and to provide meals for the artist who was leasing Orchard Cottage.

Eileen had emphasized that her bequest wasn't contingent on Caroline's compliance with her final wishes. If Caroline arranged to have Blackberry Farm put on the market as soon as the will was probated, she could leave Pleasant Valley next week. Eileen's savings and the eventual income from the farm's sale, along with Caroline's own nest egg, would give her enough money to travel through the western states, check out the territory and choose the perfect spot to put down roots.

"If you're so determined to live out west," Eileen had said in her strong gravelly voice one morning several months ago, "I don't under-stand why you haven't left long before now."

"I can't afford to."

Eileen had straightened in her rocker in her

usual ramrod posture reminiscent of royalty. Her soft gray eyes gleamed with wisdom behind silver-rimmed glasses, and every snow-white strand of her Gibson Girl hairstyle remained in place. With her face remarkably unlined and flushed with color for a woman in her nineties, she must have been a radiant beauty in her youth.

"You could have taken a job out west," Eileen said, scrutinizing her closely, "until you earned enough to buy your own place."

Caroline twisted her face into a smile that was more of a grimace. "I know everyone in town thinks I'm a wuss for putting up with my mother."

"And what do you think?"

"That there's more to it than that."

Eileen rocked gently, not commenting, waiting for Caroline to explain. Caroline grappled for the right words.

"I'm not afraid of my mother," she began, "in spite of what some people think. And I'm well aware of her faults. She's a . . . difficult woman. Has been ever since Daddy died."

"So you're not staying with her out of a sense of obligation?"

"That's a very small part of it. She is my mother, after all, and I'm her only child. I figure if I have to work until I can fulfill my dream, I might as well help her while I'm at it. Then, when the time comes, I can leave home with a clear conscience."

"And that's all?" Eileen's gaze was skeptical.

Caroline sighed. "No."

"I'm being a prying old busybody," Eileen had said with a self-deprecating laugh. "You don't owe me any explanations."

But Caroline had loved talking to her old friend. It helped her think. "Maybe I am a wuss."

"Why?"

"Because in some ways, I'm afraid to leave the valley."

"Afraid you'll miss your mother?"

Caroline shook her head. "I *know* I'll miss her, even though she drives me up the wall with her complaints and demands. She and Aunt Mona are all the family I have. But missing them is not what I'm afraid of."

Eileen nodded and rocked some more.

"What if my dream isn't all it's cracked up to be?" Caroline blurted. "What if I've spent all these years looking forward to moving out west and when I get there, I'm disappointed?"

Her friend leaned forward and grasped her hand. "It took me decades to learn one of life's most important lessons."

"Want to share?" Caroline asked. "I could use some wisdom."

With her other hand, Eileen tapped the faded blue cardigan that covered her chest. "Happiness comes from inside, from the heart. It doesn't have a thing to do with where you are. You can live in the most perfect place in the world, and if you're not content within yourself, you'll always be miserable."

"Are you suggesting I'll be miserable out west?" Caroline had asked in alarm.

Eileen had leaned back and smiled. "Quite the contrary. You've managed to be happy and content, in spite of living with your very difficult mother. I believe you'll take that happiness with you wherever you go."

Recalling that conversation, Caroline sighed.

"Thinking of your friend?" Ethan's deep, rich voice startled her. For a few moments, she'd forgotten he was there.

"Yes."

He rolled an empty glass between his broad palms before he spoke above the clamor of crickets and katydids that filled the night air. "Memories are precious, especially when they're all you have left."

His face was partially hidden in shadow, but the raw pain in his voice kept his words from sounding like platitudes. Caroline had no doubt that Ethan had experienced his own losses. But he was a temporary guest. No need to be involved with his past, even if she was curious.

She stood, intending to remove herself from the temptation of trying to learn more about him. "If you're hungry later, feel free to raid the kitchen."

He pushed to his feet and towered beside her,

the tall, dark silhouette of her afternoon dream. "Thanks for your hospitality."

Caroline struggled against the unexpected urge to lean into him, to feel the warmth of his embrace again, the soft brush of his breath against her ear, the beat of his heart beneath her cheek.

Had she lost her mind?

She attributed her uncharacteristic impulses to grief. And her uncertainty over what to do about Eileen's requests.

"Sleep well," she said.

She turned quickly and made her escape before she did something foolish, like standing on tiptoe to kiss him good-night.

For the first time in recent memory, Ethan had slept like a rock. Not a single nightmare, not one of the terrors that had stalked his dreams every night for the past few months had disturbed him. Instead of confronting the usual twisted, sweat-soaked sheets, flung pillows and a residual uneasiness, he had awakened to sunshine, bird-song and a sense of hopeful anticipation. Mercifully absent was the smothering cloud of depression that had cloaked his waking hours. After a shower and shave in the old-fashioned but spacious bathroom, he found himself humming as he dressed in jeans and T-shirt and pulled on socks and work boots.

Minutes later, lured by the aroma of freshly

brewed coffee, he entered the dining room, where a single setting at the huge table indicated he was the B and B's only guest. That fact meant he'd have more time alone with his lovely inn-keeper. The grin that had taken residence on his face since he'd awakened in such good humor widened at the prospect.

He poured himself a cup of steaming coffee from the carafe on the sideboard and settled at the table to consider his situation. Just his luck to encounter the most fascinating woman he'd ever met on the day she'd lost one of her best friends. Last night, Caroline had been understandably preoccupied. This morning, he faced the problem of how to get to know her better without intruding on her grief and looking like a jerk.

Before he could frame a solution to his dilemma, the door that led to the kitchen swung open, and Caroline, carrying a serving tray, entered the dining room. With her cheeks flushed from cooking, her blond hair gleaming in the morning sun, and a light blue denim apron embroidered with Tuttle's Bed and Breakfast covering her pale green shorts and shirt, she looked even prettier than when he'd found her yesterday, dozing in the backyard.

Bedazzled by her smile, Ethan imagined seeing such a vision every day, and the contemplation robbed him of breath.

"Sleep well?" Caroline set a plate loaded with

scrambled eggs, sausage and fluffy grits in front of him, then placed a basket of warm muffins at his elbow.

"You bet. Must be the peace and quiet. I'm used to city noises."

A closer look revealed faint shadows beneath her eyes, and a slight tremor in the hand that served his orange juice. Caroline, from the looks of her, hadn't rested well.

"Why don't you join me?" he asked. "I hate to eat alone."

Actually, lately he'd preferred his own company, but his time at the B and B was limited, and he didn't want to lose the chance to learn more about Caroline Tuttle.

His mother would be pleased.

"What you need, Ethan Garrison, is a nice girl. Settle down. Have children," had been her mantra for the last ten years. After Jerry's death, her not-so-subtle suggestions had turned to almost frantic pleas. "I'm not getting any younger. I'd like to know my grandchildren before I die."

"You wouldn't want me to marry a woman I don't love," Ethan had countered, "just to give you grandkids."

"Of course not." His mother had set her pleasant face in a pout. "But the right woman's out there, just waiting for you to come along."

"And how will I know when I've found her?" His question had been more teasing than serious.

"Far as I'm aware, even a state-of-the-art GPS is no help in locating a prospective wife."

"You'll know," his mother had insisted in poetic terms contrary to her practical nature. "Her name will sing in your soul and you won't be able to think of anything but her."

Ethan had laughed and called his mom a hopeless romantic, but watching Caroline pour herself a cup of coffee and take a seat across from him, he was beginning to understand what his mother had meant.

He buttered a warm muffin, took a bite and grinned at the burst of flavors.

"Good, huh?" Caroline said with a smile that made him want to rise from his chair and kiss her.

"So good I'd be willing to marry the woman who baked these."

Caroline laughed. "You'd have to fight off her husband first. And as a former Marine, he'd be tough to beat, even for you."

"You didn't bake these?"

She shook her head. "Jodie at the café. They're her specialty."

"What's your specialty?"

Caroline nodded toward his plate. "I wish I had a dollar for every breakfast I've cooked the past fifteen years."

"And what would you do with all that cash?"

"Buy a horse."

He almost choked on his grits. "A horse?"

She nodded and her brilliant blue eyes sparkled in the sunlight streaming through the tall east windows. "I've always wanted to learn to ride."

Caroline was nothing if not full of surprises. Most women he'd met would have wished for jewelry, designer clothes or a trip to some exotic locale. But horseback riding?

With his time with Caroline growing short, Ethan decided to take a chance. He'd never ridden a horse, but if climbing onto the back of an unfamiliar animal was what it took to make headway with the woman who captured his imagination, he'd gladly make a fool of himself. "Go riding with me today."

She considered him with a cool stare over the rim of her coffee cup. "You're not serious."

"Why not? I have a couple of days to kill. So why not spend one of them horseback riding?"

She cocked an eyebrow. "Have you ridden much?"

"Never," he admitted. "But there's always a first time."

She shook her head, but whether in astonishment or refusal, he couldn't tell.

"Is that a *no?*"

"That is most definitely a *no.*" A slight smile softened her rejection.

"Because your mama warned you not to take up with strangers?"

"Because, one, there's no place to ride horses

47

within a hundred miles, and, two, I have . . . arrangements to make."

"Your friend?"

She nodded and her smile faded, replaced by a sorrowful expression that dimmed the light in her eyes.

His opportunity was sliding away, slipping from his grasp, and he couldn't think of a damned thing to stop it. "I'm sorry."

She pressed her lips together as if fighting back tears and pushed away from the table, taking her coffee cup with her. In a moment, the kitchen door closed behind her, leaving Ethan alone to finish his breakfast and contemplate his next move. He'd be leaving tomorrow, and he was running out of time.

The following day, after a funeral attended by more than half the town and families from the outlying farms, Eileen Bickerstaff was laid to rest behind the Pleasant Valley Community Church in a cemetery plot on a rolling hill that overlooked the Piedmont River and far mountains. At the end of the service, Rand and Brynn Benedict invited the mourners to their home at River Walk for lunch.

River Walk, an impressive multistory log mansion with multiple decks that descended to the river, was the perfect spot for a crowd. Teenage boys from Archer Farm directed arriving guests to parking spots and to the buffet, catered by Jodie and set up on the largest deck beneath the shade of spreading oaks. Conversations centered on Eileen and the impact her life had made on so many people in the valley.

Caroline, wearing a sleeveless black linen dress, helped Jodie serve. Amy Lou Baker, beautician at the Hair Apparent, and Jay-Jay, the mechanic from the garage, heaped their plates and moved away to find a seat at one of the many tables Rand had rented for the event.

"Eileen was an angel," Jodie said during a lull in the buffet line. "When I was unmarried and pregnant with Brittany, an anonymous benefactor gave my parents a thousand dollars to help with my expenses. I didn't know until Rand told me yesterday that the gift came from Eileen."

Caroline nodded. "From the snippets of conversation I've heard this morning, she showed that same generosity to lots of others in the valley, too. She was a good neighbor and a good friend."

"Speaking of good friends—" Merrilee Nathan approached the buffet table "—do you two need any help?"

With her blue eyes and blond hair, Merrilee could have been Caroline's twin, except where Caroline was tall and willowy, Merrilee was full-figured and petite.

Jodie shook her head at Merrilee's offer. "Thanks, but almost everyone's been served. Why don't we fill our plates and find a table?"

Brynn left a group she'd been talking to across the deck and joined them. Her simple black dress set off her figure and complemented her deep auburn hair. When Brynn had been a cop and single, men in the valley had been known to break the speed limit, just to be pulled over by the attractive officer.

"Whenever I see you three together," Brynn said, "I figure some kind of mischief's being hatched."

"Nothing yet," Caroline said with a smile, "but maybe you'll help us think of something. Where's Jared?"

After their wedding last fall, Brynn and Rand had adopted his orphaned nephew, now an adorable if somewhat tyrannical three-year-old.

"Lillian's taking care of Jared along with Merrilee's daughter in the guest house," Brynn explained. Lillian was the Benedicts' house-keeper and nanny. "So that gives the four of us time to catch up."

Caroline settled at a table in a shady corner of the deck. Brynn, Merrilee and Jodie joined her.

"So," Brynn said, "what's happening in town?"

"What," Merrilee asked, "no new lawyer jokes?"

"The joke's on her," Jodie grinned, "marrying an attorney after all those years of lawyer-bashing."

Caroline glanced at each of her friends. "Marriage seems to agree with all of you."

"I highly recommend it." Jodie dug into her potato salad.

Caroline shrugged. "Not that I'm looking, but where would I find a husband in Pleasant Valley if I was?"

"How about right under your nose?" Brynn asked.

"What are you talking about?" Caroline toyed with the food on her plate. As delicious as it was, she'd lost her appetite when Eileen died.

"Don't you have a current guest?" Brynn said.

Jodie and Merrilee were looking at Caroline with expectation.

"He's leaving today," Caroline said. "In fact, he's probably already gone. Besides, how did you know about him?"

"I was a cop for eight years," Brynn said, "trained to observe. So when I noticed a handsome stranger wandering around town and later filling the tank of his pickup at Jay-Jay's, I made a few inquiries."

"But you're married," Caroline said.

"Married," Merrilee said with a giggle, "but obviously not blind."

"And still a cop at heart," Jodie added. "What else did you discover about Caroline's gorgeous house guest?"

"Maryland plates on his vehicle," Brynn said. "Pleasant but reserved with everyone he met in town. Didn't wear a wedding ring. Then I had to pick up Jared at day care, so my investigation was terminated."

"Well?" Jodie looked at Caroline and raised her eyebrows. "Tell us more."

"Nothing more to tell. He only stopped in the valley until the van with his furniture caught up with him. He's moving to Baltimore."

"Too bad," Brynn said. "I liked him."

"How could you?" Caroline asked in surprise. She'd drawn the same conclusion but wasn't about to admit it. "You didn't even meet him."

"Cop's intuition," Brynn said. "He was one of the good guys."

"And now he's gone," Caroline said in a tone that she hoped ended the conversation. She rose to her feet. "And I have to go, too."

"Don't leave yet," Merrilee said. "Between families and work, the four of us haven't had a chance to talk in ages."

Caroline tossed her a regretful smile. "Wish I could stay, but Eileen has a tenant arriving at Orchard Cottage tomorrow, and I promised Rand I'd check today to make sure everything's ready."

After setting a date for a girls' night out with her friends, Caroline had climbed into her old Camry for the short ride up Valley Road to the turnoff to Blackberry Farm.

Brambles, thick with almost ripe blackberries, draped the split-rail fence that lined the road to

52

the main farmhouse. Caroline slowed as she passed the old homestead, half expecting Eileen to appear on the wide front porch with a wave of welcome. The road forked just past the house, and Caroline took the left branch, a narrow red dirt road overgrown with weeds, that led to Orchard Cottage.

She parked her car in front of a picket fence in desperate need of paint and eyed the property with dismay. Eileen's tenant needed to be more than an artist. He needed to be a miracle worker. Or at least a licensed contractor, if he expected to live here. Between the sagging porch floor and missing shingles on the roof, the tiny house appeared dilapidated and sad. Caroline doubted even a good cleaning would make it presentable.

But the property was hers now, and she was embarrassed to have anyone, much less a paying tenant, view it in its present state. With a sigh of resignation, she removed a change of clothes and her bucket of cleaning materials from the car and trudged up the front walk.

Three hours later, the cottage was still derelict but clean. She had swept the floors, cleared cobwebs and scrubbed the kitchen and bathroom fixtures. She'd even washed the windows that overlooked the porch. With an ancient scythe from the barn, she'd cleared the foot-high weeds from the front yard. In an effort to make the place more welcoming, she'd filled old mason jars from the kitchen cupboard with Queen Anne's lace from the roadside and roses from the rambling bushes that grew along the fence. She placed the containers of lacy white flowers and deep red blooms on the kitchen counter and the living room windowsills. But not even the roses' cheerful color could distract from the cottage's glaring shortcomings. Caroline wondered if the poor condition of the house would be a lease-breaker. If so, the departure of her tenant would take care of one of her obligations to Eileen.

Which would still leave Caroline with the problem of what to do with little Hannah. She'd have to find just the right people to love and nurture a child who'd lost her mother.

Loading her cleaning supplies into the trunk of her car, Caroline heard the rumble of an approaching vehicle. She slammed the trunk lid and turned to see a pickup truck kicking up dust on the red dirt road. Sunlight glinted off the windshield, obscuring the driver from view. She didn't recognize the truck. It didn't belong to the Mauneys, who operated the neighboring dairy farm. Uneasiness gripped her, alone with a stranger approaching, and she headed for her car, thinking it better to be locked inside and behind the wheel with the engine running for a quick getaway when confronted by someone she didn't know.

The truck parked behind her car, and in the rearview mirror, she watched the driver's door open. First one leg swung out, clad in jeans and a work boot. Then the other leg appeared, and the driver jumped out. She recognized the Western hero of her daydreams, with his tall figure and broad shoulders silhouetted against the setting sun.

No longer afraid, she shut off the motor and climbed from her car to confront him.

"You?" he said in surprise. "I didn't expect to see you here."

Caroline's astonishment mirrored the newcomer's. "What are you doing here?"

"I stopped at the house," Ethan Garrison said, "but Mrs. Bickerstaff isn't home. I'm her new tenant."

Chapter Four

"You're a firefighter." Caroline's eyes squinted with suspicion.

"What's firefighting got to do with anything?" Ethan was trying to figure out why Caroline Tuttle was waiting at his new residence.

"I was expecting an artist."

Ethan's confusion grew. "Where's Eileen?"

Dismay flashed across her features. "You don't know?"

"Know what?"

"Are you a friend of Eileen's?"

"You might say that."

"What kind of friend? I never heard her mention you." Disbelief tinged her expression and her voice.

Ethan removed his ball cap and combed his fingers through his hair. "I met Eileen several months ago in an online chat room."

The chat room was a support group for post-traumatic stress disorder patients, but for now, that was his secret. As in AA, members kept their identities and all that was said in the online meetings confidential.

"Eileen and I," he continued, "have corresponded regularly since then. And we've talked several times recently by phone. That's how I set up the lease for this place. Eileen mailed me the papers."

"Oh, dear." Caroline, her pretty face crumpled with distress, shook her head. "I had no idea or I'd have told you that first day."

"Told me what?"

"She's gone."

"Out of town?"

"She's my friend, the one who—" Caroline struggled for words.

Ethan finally put the pieces together. "The one who died?"

Caroline nodded. "I just came from her funeral a few hours ago."

He shook his head in bewilderment. "But that's not possible."

"I'm sorry."

"You told me that your friend who died was old."

"Eileen was ninety-eight."

Stricken with sorrow and a sense of loss, Ethan sank onto the running board of his pickup. "I had no idea. She sounded so much younger in her postings and on the phone. So . . . alive."

Caroline smiled through her sadness. "That was Eileen in a nutshell."

Ethan had known that Eileen was a widow and a good bit older than he was, but he'd never guessed that she was in her nineties. When he'd confided to the support group that he needed to get away from Baltimore to try to put his life back together, she'd offered to rent her cottage with a promise of as much peace and quiet as he wanted. And she'd been savvy as well as generous. Fearing that he'd withdraw into a shell in the isolation of Orchard Cottage, she'd insisted that he share meals with her. She'd made the demand under the guise of needing company, but he'd known better. Eileen Bickerstaff had seemed too self-sufficient to need anyone.

So self-sufficient, in fact, that she'd never revealed whatever trauma had brought her to the online support group in the first place. Not that he blamed her. He hadn't been able to broach what had caused his PTSD, either. Without talking about the event and bringing his feelings into the open, his therapist had warned, Ethan couldn't expect to improve. But he hadn't found anyone he trusted well enough with whom to share his inner turmoil. He wouldn't put his family or the guys at the firehouse through the ordeal of his soul-baring—they'd all suffered enough. He'd hoped his daily face-to-face meetings with Eileen, whom he'd already considered a friend, would give him the courage to open up and express his pain and find some release.

Because he'd closed himself off from his family and his firefighting buddies, Eileen had been his only remaining friend, his one hope for an objective confidante, and now she was gone. But she had been more than a prospective sounding board. He had respected and cared for the old woman, and she'd seemed too vivacious not to have many more years ahead of her. Her unexpected death left another gaping hole in his life.

Caroline sat beside him on the running board and placed her hand on his arm. Her consoling touch was warm, her fingers long and delicate, her nails pale pink. The kind of hand he'd like to lace his fingers through and hang on tight.

"I'm sorry," she said again.

"Yeah, me, too." He cleared his throat of the emotion lodged there, rose to his feet, slapped his cap against his thigh, and placed it on his head. "Well, I guess that's that."

She stood and crossed her arms. Cocking her head at an angle, she gazed up with those amazing blue eyes that had captivated him the first day he met her. He stuck his hands in his back pockets to keep from brushing the smear of dirt from the curve of her cheek.

"What do you mean, that's that?" Caroline said.

"I'm no attorney, so, with Eileen gone, I don't know how valid my lease is, but I doubt her family will want me here. They'll probably either move in themselves or put the property on the market."

"She didn't have any family."

"No one?"

Caroline shook her head. A blue-and-white bandanna held her luxuriant blond hair away from her face. She wore cut-off jeans, sneakers green with grass stains, and a cropped top that was streaked with cobwebs and dirt.

"So what are you doing here?" he asked.

"Getting the place ready." She grimaced. "Such as it is. Eileen left me Blackberry Farm, so I'm your new landlady. That is, if you still want the place, after seeing the shape it's in."

He didn't tell her that Eileen had given him prior warning of the cottage's derelict state. One of the conditions of his lease was that he make repairs both on it and the other small house on the property. In return for his renovations, Eileen had kept his rent ridiculously low and thrown in two meals a day, because she'd known he was on a tight budget. His disability checks only went so far.

For now, Ethan was enjoying his time with Caroline so much, he wanted to extend it as long as possible, so he kept his knowledge of the property's dilapidated condition to himself. "How about showing me around so I can make up my mind?"

He swung open the gate in the rickety picket fence, made a mental note to oil the protesting hinges, and motioned Caroline ahead of him.

Luck seemed to be working in his favor for a change—and it was about time. He'd thought when he left Tuttle's Bed and Breakfast that he'd never see Caroline again, because she'd seemed so certain about her plans to head west. As sorry as he was about Eileen's death, he hoped the old woman's generous bequest would keep Caroline in the valley.

"Watch this first step," she warned as she climbed to the porch. "It's loose."

He added securing the step to his mental list and followed Caroline across the sagging porch and through the entry door. The front room was spacious and sunny with dust motes dancing in the slanting light from the western windows. Paint peeled from the walls, the hardwood floors were stained and scuffed, and several of the window-panes were cracked, but a glass jar filled with flowers stood on a windowsill, a cheerful splash of color in the otherwise dismal space. Caroline's touch, he decided, an appropriate gesture from a woman who lit up a room just by walking into it.

"Seen enough?" Caroline asked, as if expecting him to turn and run for the door.

He was staying at Orchard Cottage. He'd made up his mind as soon as Caroline had announced that she was his new landlady, and he wasn't ready for her to leave. "Might as well see it all."

Ethan followed her into the only other room on the first floor. The kitchen at the back of the house was as large as the front room with the same tall windows and lots of light. Cracked linoleum covered the floor, and an ancient porcelain sink with attached drainboard stood on spindly legs beneath a window that overlooked a gnarled apple tree in the backyard. The electric range and refrigerator were twice his age. Here, too, the paint was peeling, but someone, apparently Caroline, had scrubbed the kitchen clean. More flowers stood in a jar on the counter, a welcoming sign.

Caroline cast him a skeptical glance. "Is this what you were expecting?"

From Eileen's description, he'd expected worse. But he looked forward to working on the cottage. Staying busy helped keep his demons at bay, and he had a legion of demons, so the more work, the better.

"I've seen worse. Are the stairs safe?"

Caroline looked at him as if he'd lost his mind for even considering the place, then nodded and mounted the narrow stairs that led to the second floor. Through the residual odors of cleansers and dust, her wisteria fragrance trailed behind her, compelling him to follow her.

The stairs opened directly into one large room with tall double windows in both gables and a sloping ceiling. The closet was small, but sufficient for his needs.

"Where's the bathroom?" he asked. "And please don't tell me it's out back."

Caroline grinned and shook her head. "It's under the stairs. Like the rest of the place, it's fairly primitive."

"The house's structure seems sound. Nothing some paint and elbow grease won't fix."

"You *are* an optimist, aren't you?"

He used to be, until Jerry's death had shattered his positive outlook. Since then, Ethan had concentrated on getting through one day at a time. Now a sense of anticipation at updating the old cottage overtook him, and he experienced a twinge of his former optimism. Maybe the peaceful setting of the valley influenced his mood, but he guessed his rising spirits had more to do with the pretty woman beside him.

A woman who apparently was leaving town soon, he reminded himself, recalling their conversation on the porch after supper night before last. She'd announced today she would be his landlady, but she could fill that capacity long distance. He might find himself living in Orchard Cottage in isolation after all.

"Something wrong?" she asked.

He'd never been good at poker. His expression always gave him away, so Caroline must have read the disappointment on his face.

"Everything's fine." He flicked a wall light switch that illuminated a bare bulb in the ceiling fixture of the bedroom. "At least I have electricity."

"Rand had the power turned on, so you'd have lights and running water. I think the well pump and holding tank are in the barn."

"Rand is the lawyer who handled the lease?"

Caroline nodded. "He and his wife Brynn live at River Walk across the highway."

At least there were neighbors close by. He wouldn't be totally alone. "Let's check out the barn."

"I only had time to clean in the house, so I haven't had a good look in the barn, except to find the scythe. I have no idea what shape it's in."

The barn's condition didn't matter. The worse it was, the more work he'd have. And he'd need work, especially if he was to face his struggle here alone, without Eileen's friendship and support or the delightful company of the new owner of Blackberry Farm.

Caroline stepped onto the back porch and surveyed the rear yard of Orchard Cottage. She hadn't had time to knock down the weeds, except for the path her sneakers had trampled between the porch and the barn. Near the porch, a mockingbird trilled in an apple tree, heavy with green fruit, and bumblebees buzzed in the thick clover. The deserted chicken coop, overrun with honeysuckle, leaned at a precarious angle, and the red paint of the ancient barn had long since faded to a dusty rose.

"Wow," Ethan spoke beside her.

"Pretty bad, isn't it?"

A part of her wanted him to wash his hands of the place and head back to Baltimore or wherever he'd come from. His departure would cancel one of her obligations to Eileen. But another part recognized how nice it was to be around Ethan Garrison. She was ultra aware of the breadth of his shoulders, his killer smile—and the pain that lurked in his hazel eyes.

"Bad?" He shook his head. "It's beautiful. Like stepping back in time."

"Is that a polite way of saying 'older than dirt'?"

"No, I mean it. The place *is* beautiful. Peaceful. Exactly what I need."

Great. He liked it.

She didn't know whether to feel frustrated or pleased. Maybe the barn would be the deal-breaker. She tromped ahead, crushing the sweet clover with each step, and tugged open the barn door.

Barn swallows took flight in the hayloft, and the scurrying of tiny feet in dark corners indicated the presence of mice. Sunlight poured through the open doorway, illuminating dust, cobwebs, and tall mounds of rusting farm implements and other assorted, unrecognizable junk.

"No one has lived at Orchard Cottage for years," she explained. "Eileen used to rent the place to a family who managed the orchards, but for the last fifteen years, the Mauneys—they own the dairy farm next door—have taken care of the trees and harvested the crops."

She'd have to check with Joe Mauney to see if he'd continue that arrangement. He'd told her at the funeral that he'd already picked up Eileen's cow and placed it with his herd. The cow had to be milked twice daily, and there had been no one at Eileen's to do it. He'd offered to buy the cow, another detail to attend to before Caroline could leave the valley.

Ethan, illuminated by a sunbeam like an actor in a spotlight, stood in the middle of the floor, looking as impressed as if he'd stepped into a castle instead of a rickety barn. He cast her a satisfied grin. "This is perfect."

65

"For what? A set for a horror movie?"

He shook his head and excitement lit his hazel eyes with green flecks. "There's ample room for my equipment, and, with the hayloft doors open, plenty of good light."

"With the hayloft doors open, you'll freeze come winter."

"I can bundle up. Or buy a portable propane heater. Yes, this is definitely perfect for my studio."

"You paint?" Eileen had said her new tenant was an artist, and Caroline tried to visualize Ethan with a delicate brush in his big, scarred hands, dabbing oil paints on a canvas. Her imagination failed her.

His grin broadened, crinkling the skin around his eyes and, for an instant, chasing away the pain that had hovered there. "The only painting I'll attempt is renovating the cottage, like I promised Eileen."

"But she said you're an artist."

"I'm a sculptor."

"I see."

But she didn't. She couldn't imagine him chipping away at a block of marble or molding a statue from clay. But she could picture him in fireman's gear, rushing into a burning building to rescue its occupants. He projected the strength and calm of a go-to guy in times of trouble. Better for her if he'd been an aesthetic type instead of this paragon of masculinity. She had trouble thinking straight in his presence.

"There's lots of room for my welding equipment here." He pointed to an empty horse stall, then stuck his head into the old tack room. "And I can store scrap materials there."

"You sculpt in metal?"

"I'm a beginner, but I'm learning. Maybe someday I'll even sell something."

"So you've given up firefighting?"

His grin faded, and the pain returned to his eyes. "I'm taking a year off to try my hand as an artist. But I'm planning to return to the Baltimore City Fire Department when the year's up."

So Ethan didn't intend to settle in the valley. She breathed a sigh of relief. His stay was only temporary, and if she could find someone—maybe Mrs. Mauney—whom she could pay to feed him twice a day, once Caroline had located a loving foster family for Hannah, she could leave town with her obligations to Eileen fulfilled.

One major hurdle remained: breaking the news of her leaving to her mother. Caroline had made no secret of her intention to move west as soon as she could afford it, but Agnes had always brushed away her plans as if they were of no more importance than a bothersome fly. Her mother had never been skilled at facing reality, and Caroline's actual departure would come as a shock, probably precipitating another of her mother's frequent and infamous "spells," for which the doctors could find no cause. But Caroline refused to let her mother blackmail her with hypochondria. She'd make certain Agnes had the help she needed to run the bed-and-breakfast, but Caroline had more than fulfilled her obligations to her parent. She was leaving the valley, no matter how hard her mother might object.

Her mind whirled with the list of tasks she'd have to accomplish before her departure, the first dealing with the attractive man who was nosing through the barn, apparently unconcerned about spiders, snakes or random sharp objects. She hoped he'd had a tetanus booster.

When Ethan had arrived, he'd expected Eileen to fulfill her part of the lease and provide two meals a day, so, in the short run, Caroline felt an obligation at least to see that he was fed.

I know you'll do the right thing, dear, Eileen's voice echoed in her memory.

Caroline took a deep breath and called to him above the racket of his explorations. "You can have dinner with Mother and me and stay at our place tonight. I wasn't expecting you until tomorrow, so I haven't made any arrangements for meals at the farmhouse."

He deserted the junk he'd been sifting through and returned to her side. He seemed to sense her reluctance, which was no surprise, since her heart hadn't been in the offer.

"My furniture doesn't arrive until tomorrow, but I have a sleeping bag in the truck, and I bought a few groceries in town. I'll be fine here, but thanks for the offer."

She experienced a strange mix of disappointment and relief. She had found herself enjoying his company, but knew that her mother would pitch a fit tonight when Caroline revealed her plans. Better that the house was empty of guests when the curtain rose on that drama, one that promised to be filled with histrionics, wailing, accusations and tears.

She strode out of the barn, and Ethan followed.

"When will I see you again?" he asked.

Whether she stayed in the valley until Blackberry Farm was sold or headed west in the near future, she'd have to move out of her mother's house. If her mother followed her usual pattern when she didn't get her way, Agnes would alternate between sulks and hysterics, making Caroline's remaining time at home miserable. She'd start packing tonight and move into Eileen's house in the morning. She could launch her final move from there.

And fulfill her obligation to provide Ethan's meals until she could make other arrangements. "Come to the farmhouse for lunch tomorrow," she said, "but make it a late one. One o'clock?"

The killer smile bathed her in a warm glow. "It's a date."

"Not a date," she snapped, irritated at her rush

69

of pleasure generated by his smile. She had to get her feelings under control. "I'm honoring Eileen's wishes."

"Sure."

Undeterred by her irritation, he fell in step with her, walked her to her car and opened the door. A perfect gentleman. Why couldn't he be a resistible lout?

"Tomorrow at one," he said.

Feeling childish, bitchy and ashamed of herself for her curtness, she climbed in, started the engine, and turned the car around on the narrow dirt road. When she glimpsed Ethan in the rear-view mirror, watching her departure, hands on his lean hips, his hazel eyes narrowed under the bill of his cap, she fought the impulse to bang her head against the steering wheel.

Of course he hadn't considered lunch an actual date, dimwit. It was just a figure of speech. What was the matter with her? Too much change happening too fast, that's what. She needed to sit down, take several deep breaths, make a list and get organized. And keep her distance from the charming Mr. Garrison.

Within minutes, she reached the farmhouse, parked and went inside to inventory Eileen's pantry and refrigerator. If she had to feed her tenant until she made other arrangements, she'd need to pick up groceries when she moved from town tomorrow.

With the key Rand had provided, she let herself in. She'd expected to be overwhelmed with sadness, but was surprised to find that the house enveloped her with pleasant memories, as if Eileen's loving spirit still resided there and was welcoming her.

To her own home.

As many times as Caroline had entered Blackberry Farm, she'd never viewed it through the eyes of ownership. In her entire life, she'd never possessed a place of her own, and, even though her stay would be temporary, for now the house was all hers. With fresh appreciation, she noted the shotgun hall with its gleaming hardwood floor that reached from the front to the back door, obstructed only partly on one side by the staircase that rose to the second story with its multiple bedrooms.

On her right was the large dining room and behind it, the huge country kitchen. On the left was the spacious front parlor. Behind that, the second parlor had served for the last three decades as Eileen's bedroom, so she hadn't had to climb the stairs. It was the kind of house that had been built for a big, boisterous family, but for more than seventy years, Eileen had lived here alone. She'd come to Blackberry Farm as a bride, but her husband had died in World War II, and Eileen had never remarried. She had earned her living from the land, the acres of pasture she'd rented to the Mauneys, the profit from her orchards and the sale of her famous homemade blackberry jellies, jams, syrups and wine at a roadside stand. She'd been known throughout the valley as the Blackberry Lady.

While Eileen had been a good neighbor and well-loved, she'd had no intimate friends. In recent years, aside from Caroline, her closest relationships had been online in the various chatrooms she'd frequented.

Caroline stood in the front parlor by the computer that had been Eileen's connection to the world outside Pleasant Valley. For the first time, the enormity of the old woman's bequest hit her. This house, with its wraparound porches and two stories filled with spacious rooms, was all hers.

The irony made her laugh out loud. Finally having her own place to call home, her prevailing thought was to contact Marion Sawyer at her real estate office about putting Blackberry Farm on the market and getting out of—or, more accurately, into—Dodge.

Caroline glanced around the parlor and bedroom. Eileen, despite her advanced years, had always been as neat as a pin. Unlike many who'd lived through the Great Depression, she'd never been a hoarder or collector. Her rooms were clear of clutter and decorated in a sparse but traditional style, accented by homey touches. A crocheted afghan lay across the back of the sofa, and a handmade quilt covered the large four-poster bed, its feather pillows topped with a needlepoint throw pillow.

In many ways, for the past several years, Blackberry Farm had been more welcoming and familiar than Caroline's mother's house, where strangers came and went on a regular basis. When Caroline left Pleasant Valley, she would miss Eileen's place far more than the bed-and-breakfast.

But Caroline wasn't going anywhere soon if she didn't get busy. She hurried into the country kitchen and began an inspection of the cupboards and refrigerator. Sitting at the kitchen table, making a grocery list, she heard a vehicle head up the road from the highway.

She strode to the living room window and peeked out. A pickup truck with the Archer Farm logo on the door parked behind her car, and Jack Hager, Archer Farm's resident psychologist, hopped out and headed up the front walk. With his hair the color of cornsilk, pale blue eyes and the gold-rimmed glasses he sometimes wore, Gofer, as his friends called him, would have looked like a college professor—except for the rest of him. In his fitted olive-drab T-shirt, shorts and work boots, the uniform of Archer Farm, he looked one-hundred-and-ten percent United States Marine.

Caroline stepped onto the front porch to greet him.

"I was hoping you'd still be here," he said. "Brynn said you were stopping by to get ready for your new tenant."

"What can I do for you?"

He waved an accordion folder in his right hand. "Some papers to sign. Just a formality."

"Papers?"

"For Hannah's guardianship. I have to turn them in to social services before Hannah arrives on Monday."

Caroline racked her brain for a way to break the news that she wasn't taking Hannah. Gofer looked so pleased, she hated to let him down standing on the front walk. "It's hot out. How about a glass of tea?"

"You don't have to twist my arm. The boys and I have been working hard, taking down tables and chairs from the luncheon at River Walk and carting them back to the church. It's hot enough in town to fry an egg on the pavement."

He followed her into the house and down the hall to the kitchen. Still trying to decide how to tell him she couldn't take Hannah, Caroline filled the teakettle and set it on the gas burner with easy familiarity. She knew Eileen's kitchen as well as her mother's. While she placed tea bags in a pot and took sugar from the cabinet, Gofer sat at the table and removed a sheaf of papers from his folder.

She couldn't help thinking how relaxed she felt

with him, even though he was drop-dead handsome. When she was around Gofer, her heart rate didn't increase and her palms didn't sweat. Like most of the other men she knew in the valley, Gofer seemed like an older brother, a man she admired and regarded with affection. Unlike Ethan Garrison in whose presence she felt like an awkward adolescent.

"How'd you get the name Gofer?" she asked, stalling for time.

"My Marine buddies christened me. My favorite expression is 'go for broke,' which they shortened to Gofer."

"Funny saying for a psychologist."

"I don't know." He cocked his head, and late afternoon sunlight glinted off the lenses of his glasses. "A lot of people miss out on a great deal in life because they don't have the courage to go after what they want. A good counselor can help them recognize that."

He'd given her the opportunity she'd been looking for. "Eileen's given me the chance to live my dream."

"Blackberry Farm?"

Caroline nodded. "But not in the way you think. I'm going to sell the place and use the money to move out west."

He looked surprised. "Not soon, I hope."

"I'm planning to leave in a couple of weeks."

"But what about Hannah?"

"I'll help you locate another foster family."

His expression bleak, Gofer shook his head. "Not possible."

"Never thought I'd hear a Marine utter those words," Caroline said with a smile. "Don't you guys do the impossible every day?"

He didn't return her smile. "Hannah's mother died before Easter. I've been searching for months for an appropriate foster family. I'd hit a dead end when Eileen stepped forward. Her age was problematic, but her proximity to the farm and Daniel was a real plus. If you don't take Hannah, it could be months again before I find someone."

"Months? But I'm leaving sooner than that."

"For an adult, months pass quickly." He opened the folder, removed a photograph and slid it across the table toward her. "But months can seem like years when you're nine, especially when you've recently lost your mother and your only living relative is miles away."

With reluctance Caroline picked up the color photograph. A tiny girl, with looks that central casting for a production of *Annie* would love, stared back at her. Hannah had a gamin face, a riot of short red curls, wide blue eyes and an aura of dejection and loss that clutched at Caroline's heart. "She's precious, but she looks so sad."

"Look at those eyes. She's experienced too much unhappiness for one so young. Deserted as an infant by her father, raised by her alcoholic mother, an orphan at nine. The girl's seen too much turmoil and heartache and not enough love."

Caroline couldn't drag her gaze from the little girl's photo. "Those same circumstances got her brother into trouble."

Gofer nodded. "I'll admit that the odds are against Hannah. Without the right guidance and love, she'll end up a statistic and either in juvenile detention or abused, an unwed mother, a thief, a prostitute, hooked on drugs—the dire possibilities are endless."

Caroline couldn't match any of the horrible outcomes Gofer was predicting with the compelling innocence in the little girl's face. She set down the photo, poured boiling water over the tea bags, and filled two glasses to the brim with ice. The little girl with the desolate expression had awakened strong maternal feelings Caroline hadn't known she possessed. Those emotions vied with her impatience to fulfill her dream.

"What if I do take her? I don't plan to stay in the valley long. Being bounced from one home to another has to be traumatic for a kid. Isn't it better to leave her where she is until you can find a permanent place?"

Gofer leaned back in his chair, folded his muscular arms over his chest and shot her a grim look. "She's in a foster home in Greenville with seven other children. Not exactly the best of circumstances for a grieving child, or any child, for that matter."

Caroline added sugar to the hot tea, stirred it, then poured the steaming mixture over ice in the glasses and handed one to Gofer. All the while, Hannah's sorrowful eyes, her photo burned indelibly into Caroline's brain, confronted her.

I know you'll do the right thing, dear, Eileen's voice echoed again in her mind.

If only I knew what the right thing was.

Caroline took her glass of tea and sat across the broad pine table from the psychologist. "I'm leaving the valley, if not in a few weeks, at least in a month or so. It seems cruel to take Hannah for such a short while, then move her again."

He drank his tea, then nodded. "On the other hand, while you're here, she'd have your undivided attention, she'd be close to her brother, and she'd be settling into a caring community where she'd remain after you leave."

"So you're saying I should take her?"

Gofer smiled and shook his head. "This is your decision."

"But you're a psychologist. I thought you guys knew all the answers."

"A good counselor doesn't tell people what to do. He helps them explore their options."

Caroline stripped off her bandanna and pushed her fingers through her hair. "Everything—Eileen's death, her bequest, including a new tenant and a foster child—it's all happening too fast. I'm in over my head and going under for the last time."

Gofer leaned forward, his expression kind, his eyes earnest behind his gold-rimmed glasses. "I will give you one piece of advice."

"Please. I need all the help I can get."

"Don't decide anything now. Sleep on it tonight."

Caroline managed a weak grin. After she informed her mother that she was moving out tomorrow, she doubted she'd get any sleep tonight at all.

Chapter Five

Caroline tucked the sack of groceries under her arm and struggled to unlock the front door of the farmhouse with her other hand. Her premonition of a sleepless night had proved to be dead-on. Her brain felt fogged, her feet heavy as lead, and her nerves frazzled over her dilemma of what to do about Blackberry Farm, Hannah and one too-handsome former firefighter. Not to mention the monumental hissy fit her mother had thrown at Caroline's announcement of moving out. For two cents, she'd chuck her responsibilities, climb into her ancient Toyota and head west—except, in its present state, the car probably wouldn't make it through Tennessee.

"Want some help?" a deep voice boomed behind her.

Startled, she lost her grip on the grocery bag. It hit the porch floor, ripped down one side, and scattered its contents across the painted boards.

Clutching her pounding heart, she whirled to find Ethan on his knees, scurrying after a lemon before it rolled off the edge of the porch.

"Sorry," he called over his shoulder. "I didn't mean to frighten you."

She felt like an idiot. If she hadn't been so stressed-out after the confrontation with her mother and a night without sleep, maybe she wouldn't have reacted so skittishly. Recognizing her handsome tenant, however, didn't calm her nerves.

"I didn't hear your truck," she said, breathing deep and hoping for her pulse to slow. "You came out of nowhere and scared me to death."

He snagged the last of the items, tucked them into the remnants of the sack, and pushed to his feet. His smile was 250-watt and apologetic. "My truck's back at Orchard Cottage."

"Engine trouble? I can call Jay-Jay at the garage."

He shook his head. "I'm on foot by choice. Thought I'd take a stroll and get a look around the place while I'm waiting for my furniture. I've never seen so many blackberries. They're growing like kudzu along every fence. Looks like they're almost ripe."

She took the bag of groceries he held. "Eileen always loved blackberry-picking. Said it was her favorite time of year."

He glanced over his shoulder toward her parked car and nodded toward her open trunk. "Need a hand?"

An automatic *no* sprang to her lips, but she bit it back. She was dead tired, her back ached from hauling boxes downstairs from her bedroom and into the car, and she'd be foolish not to take advantage of the muscle being offered.

"Thanks."

He sprinted down the porch steps, glanced into the trunk, then back at her. "Does everything come inside?"

She hesitated. Moving all her belongings into the farmhouse seemed too much like a long-term commitment, but she had yet to decide what she planned to do.

"Put the boxes of books in the living room, please." She would leave them packed, ready for the next move. "Clothes go upstairs in the first bedroom on the left."

She wouldn't use Eileen's bedroom but one of the upstairs rooms. *If* Hannah came, Caroline couldn't make her sleep in a room on a floor all by herself. The child would be frightened enough in the big, strange house without being isolated on the second story. She'd want Caroline close by.

Caroline carried the groceries into the kitchen and began putting them away. She couldn't believe she was considering taking the little girl in, even for a short time. But Hannah's picture, left prominently by Gofer in the middle of the pine table, stared up at her, the child's unhappiness almost palpable. Who wouldn't want to put a smile on that precious face?

Caroline remembered her own childhood, the happy carefree years filled with the love of her parents. Agnes had been a better mother, warmer, less anxious and less self-centered, before her husband's death. In addition, Caroline had enjoyed the companionship of good friends and the feelings of kinship and belonging in the close-knit community of Pleasant Valley. She'd never been scared, never gone hungry, never been abandoned by her parents. Sure, she'd had to take control after her father died, when her mother had fallen apart and hadn't been able to put the pieces back together. But by that time, Caroline had been an adult with the self-confidence and skills needed to face the task.

How prepared was a nine-year-old to face life with no one she could lean on, no one to protect her, no one to offer hugs and kisses and assurances that the world wasn't such a terrible place?

"All done." Ethan stood in the doorway.

Caroline blinked. How long had she been

standing there, lost in thought? "You unloaded the entire car?"

"Except for the spare tire and the jack," he said with a grin.

And the man hadn't even broken a sweat. In a navy blue T-shirt emblazoned in gold with BCFD, he looked as crisp and cool as if it were late October instead of a ninety-degree late June day.

"Thanks for your help. Would you like something to drink?"

"Anything cold would be good."

Caroline removed the pitcher of tea she'd made yesterday from the refrigerator, filled two glasses with ice, and added the golden liquid.

Ethan stepped inside the kitchen to take the glass she offered, and his gaze fell on the photograph in the center of the table.

"Who's this?"

"A long story."

He shrugged. "I'm just waiting for the moving van to show up. A long story would fill the time."

Caroline started to protest that she had a million things to do, then reconsidered. Ethan could lend an objective ear, and she could use all the advice she could get. Someone somewhere had to have an answer to the conundrum that faced her.

With a glass of iced tea in hand, Ethan followed Caroline onto the broad front porch, where, as she'd promised, the shade of the overhang and a cool breeze blowing off the mountains provided relief from the summer heat. She settled into the old-fashioned porch swing, and, as much as he wanted to sit beside her, he took the nearest white rocker with its green-and-white gingham cushion.

"So who's the little girl?" He pointed to the photo she'd brought with her.

"Hannah. Her mother died last spring, and Eileen had agreed to be her foster parent, so Hannah could be near her brother Daniel, her only remaining relative, who lives at Archer Farm."

"The rehabilitation center for boys Eileen told me about?"

Caroline nodded.

"That must be the short version."

"What?"

"Of the long story you were going to tell me."

She looked so distressed, he had to muster all his self-control to keep from moving next to her and taking her in his arms.

"Eileen had a feeling she wouldn't be able to fulfill that commitment," Caroline said, "so before she died, she left a letter, asking me to take Hannah."

His heart sank at the implications in her words and tone of voice. "Which you can't do because you're moving out west."

"Exactly."

"But you're obviously not happy about it."

"About moving? It's what I've dreamed of for almost fifteen years."

"Then why the long face?"

"Because there's no one else to take Hannah."

"What about Rand, the attorney, and his wife? The ones who live across the highway?"

"They're newlyweds. And they just adopted Rand's orphaned nephew, Jared. Even if Rand and Brynn were okay with fostering Hannah, Jared doesn't need any more changes to adjust to right now. He's only three."

"Any other neighbors?"

"The Mauneys. But they're up in years. Good people, but somewhat dour. I don't know how they'd adjust to a nine-year-old, or vice versa. Hannah's life to this point has been dismal. She needs a more upbeat atmosphere."

"And there's no one at Archer Farm who could take her?"

"Jodie and Jeff—he's the executive director—have their hands full with the resident boys and Jodie's teenage daughter Brittany. Not to mention that a facility for delinquent teens isn't the best surroundings for a fragile child."

"Maybe someone in town—"

"Gofer—Archer Farm's psychologist—has tried everyone." Her deep blue eyes glistened with unshed tears. "I'm caught between a rock and a hard place. I've waited so long to fulfill my dream, but how can I abandon a little girl who has no one?"

"Maybe I could take her." The words tumbled out unexpectedly. Like Caroline, his heart had been touched by Hannah's sad face.

"You?"

"Don't look so surprised. I have a kid sister. And I have lots of memories of when Amber was nine. She was a wild child as I recall, but Jerry and I—" he coughed to cover up the embarrassing break in his voice at his brother's name "—we loved her to pieces."

Caroline appeared to consider his offer, then shook her head. "Despite your big brother experiences, I doubt social services would place a young girl with a single male. And a girl that age needs a mother figure."

"You're right." His offer had been impulsive and unrealistic, and he was relieved at its rejection, even though he felt for Hannah, whose expression in her photo made her appear so unhappy and vulnerable. "So you're back to square one."

Caroline propped her elbows on her knees and buried her face in her hands. "Why can't life be simple?"

"It seldom is." Ethan knew that fact too well. His life the past few months had been filled with excruciating loss, physical and emotional pain, and a heavy burden of guilt. Like Caroline, he was searching for simplicity, the main reason he'd come to Pleasant Valley, but he'd found instead one complication after another: first, the discovery of a woman who'd made him feel alive again, then the unexpected death of his friend. And now, to his disappointment, the woman who'd revived his numbed psyche was determined to leave town.

Caroline sat up and stared out across the deep-pink crepe myrtles blooming profusely in the lush green lawn. "I don't know what to do."

"What did your mother suggest?" Ethan had met Agnes Tuttle at the bed and breakfast. She'd seemed like a kind woman, although a bit ditzy, unlike her capable and down-to-earth daughter.

Caroline frowned. "Mother was no help. Once I told her I was moving out, she dissolved into hysterics. I had to call Dr. Anderson to prescribe her a sedative."

"She didn't know about your plans to move out west?"

"Mother knew, all right. She was just counting on them never happening."

Thinking back to his stay at the Tuttles', Ethan recalled that Caroline had done all the work. Her mother Agnes had hovered, playing hostess, but never lifted a finger to help. "Is she worried about running the bed-and-breakfast on her own?"

"I've already hired Rosa Ortega to help out. Mother's mainly upset because she can't run my life any longer." Caroline clapped her hand over her mouth and her eyes widened. "I can't believe I said that."

"Is it true?"

Caroline nodded. "Don't get me wrong. I love my mother, but I'm not blind to her faults. She's manipulative and self-centered, has been ever since my father died. It's how she coped with missing him." She fell back in the swing and shook her head. "And why I'm confessing to a stranger what I'd never admit to anyone in town I have no idea."

"It's like sitting next to someone on a plane or a bus. You figure you'll never see them again—" he felt a twinge of sadness at those words "—so you can speak without censoring."

He finished the last of his tea and set his glass on a wicker side table. "Maybe your mother could take Hannah. Then she wouldn't be so lonely with you gone."

Caroline narrowed her eyes, thought for a moment, then shook her head. "Nope. Wouldn't work. Since Daddy died, Mama's forgotten how to give. In her grief and fear, she became too needy. Hannah needs nurturing. Mama was great while I was growing up, but now she's no longer capable of providing what a lonely child needs."

Caroline stretched her legs and gazed at him with bottomless blue eyes. "Do you think I'm awful? Talking about my own mother like that?"

He shook his head. "Not awful, just perceptive. It's hard to reach such objectivity about the people you're closest to."

"Eileen deserves the credit for any insight I

have." Her smile softened when she mentioned her late friend. "Heaven knows, she listened to enough of my griping over the years. And she taught me how to put people and things in perspective. I wish she were here now to advise me on Hannah."

"If Eileen were here, Hannah wouldn't be your problem."

Caroline gazed out across the front lawn with her forehead wrinkled in worry.

"What's your hurry?" he asked.

She jerked around to face him. "Hannah will be here in four days!"

"That's not what I meant. What's your hurry to leave Pleasant Valley?"

Her delicate nostrils flared with indignation. "I've been waiting almost fifteen years. I wouldn't call my desire to get out a stampede."

The cowboy term made him smile. "Have you picked out your new home?"

She spread her arms against the back of the swing, and pushed off with her toe. The chains creaked as the swing swayed. "I haven't even chosen which state I want to live in yet, but I'm leaning toward New Mexico."

He raised his eyebrows in surprise. "I thought you had a plan."

She shook her head, and a pale pink flush crept up her neck and into her cheeks. "Only generally speaking. I don't want to make specific plans yet.

Having a particular place in mind would make waiting to leave even harder."

"So why don't you take time to do your research? You can check out almost everything online. Narrow your options. Maybe take a few short trips to check things out. And in the meantime, you could get Blackberry Farm ready to sell. Make it a showplace. Repairing the cottages is one of the terms of my lease. The more I have completed, the better price you'll get."

She frowned, and he feared he'd offended her. What right did he have to butt into her business, anyway? As far as she was concerned, he was a stranger she'd never see again, someone with a lot of nerve to suggest what she ought to do.

Just when he'd decided he should leave her alone with her dilemma, she smiled with the brilliance of the sun coming from behind a cloud.

"You're right." Her face lighted with a healthy glow that accentuated her beauty. "I'd been planning to strike out and travel where the spirit moved me, but what you're suggesting has its good points."

Encouraged, he added, "And you can keep Hannah in the meantime—"

"—and search for another foster family for when I leave." The worry lines on her forehead had completely faded.

"You've already done the hardest part," he said.

90

"I have?"

"Making the break with your mother."

Caroline scowled. "We're just a few miles from town, and there's only the telephone and a good road between us. Mama will be burning up the highway and the phone lines once she's over her initial shock, begging me to come home."

"You can handle her. Eileen's given you this marvelous opportunity. She wouldn't want you to waste it."

Caroline nodded thoughtfully. "You give good advice."

He shrugged, but her comment pleased him. "It's always easier to come up with answers to someone else's problems."

She slanted her head and looked at him with an intensity that made him uncomfortable. For a moment, he expected her to ask what his problems were, but she rewarded him instead with another dazzling smile.

"Now that we have Hannah settled for the time being, how about that lunch I promised you?"

Chapter Six

The following evening, Caroline relaxed in a corner booth in the back of Ridge's Barbecue where she'd come for her girls' night out with Jodie, Brynn and Merrilee. All four were devouring

Ridge's famous ribs, coleslaw, hush puppies and French fries.

Only yesterday Caroline had moved out of her mother's house, and the intoxicating sense of freedom was going to her head. If not for the heavy responsibilities that tethered her firmly to the ground, she'd be flying.

Jodie raised her glass. "Let's toast Caroline's newfound independence. I thought this day would never come, but I'm happy for you. No more slaving away at the B and B. You're on your own now, girlfriend."

The others lifted their glasses and clinked them together. "To Caroline's new adventures."

Caroline raised her glass. "To Eileen, who made it all possible."

"To Eileen," they said in unison.

Brynn licked barbecue sauce from the corner of her mouth and fixed Caroline with a piercing look. "So? When are you going to tell us?"

Caroline blinked. "Tell you what?"

Brynn shook her head. "When are you going to tell us about your new tenant?"

Caroline wasn't sure she wanted to share her thoughts about Ethan Garrison, especially since she hadn't figured out exactly what those thoughts were.

"The artist?" she hedged.

"What artist?" Merrilee asked.

"Eileen rented Orchard Cottage before she died," Caroline explained, "to an artist."

"And?" Brynn prodded.

"And he moved in yesterday."

Her companions had stopped eating and were watching her closely.

"Aren't you forgetting a few salient details?" Brynn asked.

Jodie raised her eyebrows. "Who is this artist?"

"Ethan Garrison," Caroline said.

Merrilee leaned back against the bench with a grimace. "We need more than a name. Is he nice? How old is he? What does he look like?"

Caroline was trying to decide how much to divulge when Brynn, her eyes shining with mischief, spoke up. "He's a former firefighter from Baltimore. About Caroline's age. Handsome as sin. Sculpts in metal. And will be having lunch and dinner with Caroline every day."

Jodie's eyes widened. "The good-looking guy who was staying at the bed-and-breakfast earlier in the week?"

Brynn nodded. "One and the same."

Caroline felt her jaw drop. "How do you know all that? I thought Rand kept his client's business confidential."

"He does. Rand is a professional whose lips are sealed." Brynn's devilish grin widened. "So I sent in my undercover agent."

"Who?" Jodie asked.

"Lillian. She heard from Mrs. Mauney that we have a new neighbor at Orchard Cottage, so she baked a cake and took it over this afternoon. Lillian would have found out more—she's a great listener—but he was busy unpacking, so she got out of his way."

Merrilee turned to Caroline and shook a sauce-stained finger at her. "You have a gorgeous tenant you're cooking for and you didn't tell us?"

"I haven't exactly had a chance. You guys are doing all the talking. Besides, Ethan's being there is irrelevant. As soon as I find a home for Hannah—"

"Whoa! Back up," Merrilee said. "Now I'm really confused. Who's Hannah?"

"Daniel's little sister," Jodie volunteered. "Their mother died, and Eileen was going to foster Hannah so she could be near her brother."

Merrilee's blue eyes lighted in admiration. "Wow, Caro, I have to give you credit. You may wait to make your moves, but when you finally act, you don't mess around. Leaving home and getting a man and a little girl, all at once. Making up for lost time, sugar?"

"I don't have a man, I have a *tenant*. And I need to find a foster family for Hannah before I leave."

"Leave?" the three shouted, loud enough to be heard above the conversations of the restaurant's other customers and the wail of Keith Urban on the jukebox.

"You're not staying at Blackberry Farm?" Jodie

asked with a frown. "I was looking forward to having you as a neighbor."

"Me, too," Merrilee said. "You're not really leaving the valley?"

Her friends' distress warmed her heart and made her recognize for the first time how sorely she would miss these women in her life. "I'm moving out west."

"You're serious?" Brynn said. "You've always talked about buying a ranch, but I thought that was just a fantasy."

"I'm serious," Caroline insisted.

"How can you leave the valley?" Merrilee asked.

"You're a fine one to ask," Caroline said with a smile to soften her words. "You're the one who took off to New York City for six whole years."

Merrilee flushed. "Yes, but I discovered what I wanted was here all along."

"You mean Grant," Jodie said. "My brother's a great guy, if I do say so myself."

Merrilee nodded. "Grant, my parents, my friends, the town. I was crazy to leave this place. I'm glad Sophia will be growing up here." Sophia was Grant and Merrilee's six-month-old daughter, named after her paternal grandmother. "The world's a scary place these days, but the valley remains this island of calm in the midst of a storm."

"Maybe you need to experience the storm to appreciate the calm," Caroline said. "Although the kind of place I have in mind is a lot like the valley. A tiny ranch in a peaceful rural setting, surrounded by mountains."

"Sounds like Blackberry Farm," Jodie said.

"But there're no cowboys at Blackberry Farm," Caroline said with a dramatic sigh.

Brynn laughed. "Who needs a cowboy when you have a hunky firefighter?"

Caroline sighed in frustration. "I don't *have* a hunky firefighter." But she couldn't help grinning. "I have hunky *tenant*."

Jodie lifted her glass of water. "Glad to see you haven't lost your eye for a good-looking man."

"What I need," Caroline said, "is a foster mother for Hannah, so I can sell the farm and make my move."

"I'd take her," Jodie said, "but I'm going to have my hands full."

"You already have your hands full," Brynn began, then stopped and eyed Jodie closely. "You passed on the coffee."

Jodie nodded with an uncharacteristic flush. "No caffeine for me. Not for the next seven months."

"You're pregnant?" Merrilee threw her arms around Jodie for a bone-crushing hug. "That's great. Sophia will have a playmate close by."

"Jeff's hoping for a boy." Jodie glowed with pleasure and good health.

"He already has sixteen teenage boys," Caroline said.

"And four overgrown ones who call themselves Marines," Brynn added.

Happy tears glistened in Jodie's eyes. "But none of them call Jeff Daddy."

Realizing she wouldn't be here when Jeff and Jodie's baby arrived, Caroline felt a pang of regret. The West might hold all kinds of adventures and new friends, but none like these women whom she'd known as long as she could remember.

As if reading her thoughts, Jodie reached for her hand and squeezed. "You'll have to fly home for the christening."

Caroline nodded. "With Mama running a bed-and-breakfast, I'll always have a place to stay when I visit."

Later, when Caroline climbed out of Jodie's van at Blackberry Farm, she heard the purr of a well-tuned engine. Headlights sliced through the darkness on the road from Orchard Cottage, and the car slowed as it reached the main farmhouse. Rand rolled down the window of his Jaguar and waved before continuing toward the highway.

"Wonder where he's been?" Jodie said.

"Probably answering Ethan's questions about how Eileen's death affects his lease."

"It's eleven o'clock."

Caroline shrugged, but she was more curious than she let on. "They could have been watching a baseball game."

Jodie nodded. "Male bonding with the new neighbor." She sighed. "Living in close proximity to all that teen and Marine testosterone, I've become an expert on male bonding."

"Thanks for the ride," Caroline said. "And I'm really happy about your baby."

"Sure you won't stick around until he arrives?"

"What?" Caroline teased. "Need another sitter close by?"

Jodie shook her head. "Another friend. I was really looking forward to you being my nearest neighbor."

"I'll come back to visit."

"But it won't be the same as having you here every day, to run into town with or come up for coffee."

"I never had time for either while I was working for Mama." The prospect of socializing was appealing, but Caroline was determined that nothing—not friendships, not tenants, not a nine-year-old orphan—would change her plans.

Jodie gazed at her through the open van window, her face visible in the bright moonlight and the lights from the dash. "Don't burn your bridges."

Caroline shook her head. "You'll always be my friend."

"You bet, but that's not what I meant. Don't sell the farm."

"How else can I afford to buy a ranch?"

"Rent this place out for a while first. That way,

if things don't work out in cowboy land the way you hope, you'll have a home to come back to."

"Why wouldn't things work out? Moving west is what I've always wanted."

"What if you get lonesome in the wide-open spaces?"

"I'll be okay."

Caroline had always been the most solitary of her friends, partly because of the demands of the bed-and-breakfast, but also by temperament. Often a good book was all the company she needed. But being alone was different when she was surrounded by friends and family. How would she feel in a new place where she had no one?

Jodie put the van into reverse. "What's important is that you're doing what you've always wanted. But we'll still miss you."

"I'll be around for a while. We'll get together again soon."

"Call me." Jodie waved goodbye, backed into the road and headed for the highway.

Ethan stood on the porch in a rectangle of light from the open front door and watched the taillights of Rand's Jaguar disappear down the narrow dirt road. The lawyer's appearance at his house several hours earlier had taken him by surprise.

Ethan had been unpacking boxes in the kitchen when a knock had sounded on the door. Probably another neighbor with a cake or covered dish. Pleasant Valley with its friendly population had no need for a welcoming committee.

Ethan had gone to the front entrance to find a tall, dark-haired stranger, dressed in jeans and a Clemson University T-shirt, with a large pizza box in his hands, standing on the other side of the screen.

"Welcome to Pleasant Valley," the stranger said with a friendly grin. "I'm Rand Benedict. Lillian said you were settling in, so I brought dinner—or supper, as they call it in these parts."

"I'm Ethan." He opened the door for Rand to step inside. "But you already knew that."

Rand nodded. "I got your call on my office voice mail. No need to worry about your lease. Orchard Cottage is yours for as long as you want it." He hefted the pizza box. "You want this in the kitchen?"

"Sure. Will you join me?"

"I was hoping you'd ask. My wife Brynn is eating out with her girlfriends."

"With Caroline? She offered to fix my supper, but I told her not to bother if she was going out."

"Brynn's with Caroline, Jodie Davidson and Merrilee Nathan. The men in this valley are in big trouble when those four put their heads together." From the affection in his voice when he mentioned his wife and her friends, Rand seemed more amused than worried about the women's meeting.

Ethan followed him into the kitchen, took the pizza box, and set it on the large pine table next to Lillian's chocolate pound cake and Mrs. Mauney's peach cobbler. "We're all set for dessert."

"The women in this valley will feed you till you pop, if you let them. But what a way to go. I've never met so many great cooks in one place, except New York City. You're a lucky man. Caroline can cook up a storm. Two meals a day with her, and in a few weeks, you'll be needing bigger clothes."

Ethan relished the prospect of that much time with Caroline and silently thanked Eileen for providing him the opportunity. He'd need to work fast, though, with Caroline bent on leaving. He glanced up to find Rand observing him closely.

"I won't gain weight with all the work I need to do around this place," he said quickly and turned to the stack of boxes he'd yet to unpack. "Now, which one has the plates?"

"Forget plates." Rand grabbed a roll of paper towels off the counter. "These'll do fine. Help yourself to pizza. Fresh from the freezer to Lillian's oven to you."

Ethan selected a slice of pizza smothered with melted cheese and pepperoni. "I guess delivery pizza is one of the sacrifices of country living."

"Yeah, but it's worth it." Rand straddled a chair,

took a bite of pizza, chewed and swallowed. "I feel ten years younger since leaving the city. Life's slower here, the people friendlier. It's easier to keep your priorities straight."

Ethan opened the nearest box and searched for a knife to slice the pizza. "Great company and pizza. Nothing wrong with your priorities."

Later, sitting with Rand on the back porch and listening to the Yankees-Red Sox game on the radio, Ethan swatted a mosquito and raised the question he'd been itching to ask all evening. "So, have you known Caroline long?"

Rand, his face illuminated by the light streaming from the kitchen window, raised an eyebrow. "I met her last year while she was working for Eileen. Why?"

Ethan shrugged, unwilling to divulge how Caroline had fascinated him from the first moment he'd seen her. "Just wondering what kind of landlady she'll be."

"Caroline is as sweet-tempered as they come," Rand said with obvious approval, "although how Agnes Tuttle produced such a good-natured child is a miracle. Agnes is infamous for her sharp tongue and busybody meddling."

"I met Mrs. Tuttle when I stayed at the bed-and-breakfast. She seemed nice enough."

"Until you cross her. I'm sure she gave Caroline hell for abandoning her."

"Abandoning? By moving out? Caroline's a grown woman and Agnes looks like the type who can take care of herself."

Rand stretched his long legs in front of him, crossed them at the ankle, and took a slow drink of iced tea. "Agnes uses illness as an excuse to keep Caroline at her beck and call. No wonder her only daughter wants to move to the other side of the country. That's the only way she'll get away from her mother."

"Caroline does seem enthralled by all things Western," Ethan said. "I caught a look at her book collection when I was unloading boxes for her yesterday. Zane Grey, Louis L'Amour, Larry McMurtry. And lots of DVDs of Westerns. She must like cowboys."

"Which reminds me." Rand reached behind him and tugged an envelope from his back pocket. "Thought you might want these. A client gave them to me, but Brynn and I have plans for that evening already. Maybe you can get Caroline to go with you."

Ethan took the envelope and extracted four tickets to a rodeo at the Bi-Lo Center in Greenville. Rand's gesture was generous, but Ethan wasn't sure he wanted to fan the flames of Caroline's obsession. "Thanks."

Rand must have heard the hesitation in his tone. "You like rodeos?"

"Don't know. Never attended one."

But, on second thought, maybe the rodeo wasn't such a bad idea after all. If he could make headway with Caroline, he'd gladly sit through an opera, even though he hated the art form, so a rodeo would be a piece of cake by comparison. But taking her to a rodeo could backfire, sharpening her appetite for moving west and accelerating her timetable. What Ethan really wanted was to persuade her to remain in the valley. He needed time. Not for himself. All the time in the world wouldn't change his mind. Or his heart. He'd known from the day he met her that Caroline was the woman for him. He wanted her in his life, every day, for as long as he lived. But so far Caroline appeared oblivious to him, except for her awareness of her obligation to feed him twice a day. He wanted time to make her fall in love with him. Then, if she still wanted to leave the valley, he'd take her back to Baltimore. Or even move out west with her.

How can you ask Caroline to share your life when you're a walking disaster?

But he didn't intend to remain an emotional wreck. He'd come to the valley to pull himself together. Caroline provided a great incentive to overcome the trauma that had devastated him.

"Hannah will be here by then," Rand observed, nodding at the rodeo tickets. "Maybe you could take her and Daniel, too. Give the kids a chance to be together."

"Great idea. Thanks."

Ethan was counting on Hannah. If the little girl was as lovable as her picture portrayed, Caroline would be a goner once she met the child. Ethan was hoping Hannah would win Caroline's heart, make her reluctant to turn the little girl over to someone else, and cause Caroline to delay her departure. Because the longer Caroline remained at Blackberry Farm, the more time Ethan would have to . . . to what? How could he make her fall for him?

He needed time and he needed patience. And he needed somehow to figure out what on earth he was doing.

The morning after Rand's visit, Ethan still didn't have a plan to capture Caroline's interest. He'd spent another night filled with terrors and flashbacks and awoke determined to conquer the demons that had haunted him all night. Staying busy was his best weapon.

Standing on the back porch with his morning coffee in hand, he surveyed the backyard of Orchard Cottage. An unsightly compost heap, head-high and covered with scraggly weeds, occupied one side of the picturesque barn and marred the rustic beauty of his view. As soon as he'd had breakfast, he'd clear the area, start another compost pile out of sight of the back porch, and prepare the leveled site to plant spring bulbs come fall. As a child, he'd helped his mother in her garden, and she'd taught him well. With a little effort, he could turn not only Orchard Cottage but also its surroundings into a showplace.

And the physical activity would keep him from remembering and help him think of what to do about Caroline.

Breakfast could wait, he decided. He downed his coffee, set his cup on the rail and headed to the barn to search for a wheelbarrow and shovel.

Saturday morning, Caroline sat at the kitchen table. Sunlight streamed through the east window, a cup of her favorite tea steamed at her elbow and the melodies of songbirds were the only sounds that broke the peaceful stillness. Caroline, however, didn't feel peaceful. Now that she'd made the break with her mother, she itched to continue her journey. She'd moved west, she thought with a wry smile, but only by ten miles. She had a long way to go to fulfill her dreams.

But first she had to fulfill her obligations to Eileen. She stared at the blank pad and pencil on the table. She'd intended to make a list of prospective foster parents for Hannah, but she had come up with only one name, Amy Lou Baker, owner of the Hair Apparent. A middle-aged widow with a good heart, Amy Lou had a lot of love to give, but not much time. Her beauty shop was open six days a week and kept her busy. And

Caroline had no idea if Amy Lou would want the responsibility of a nine-year-old.

After Amy Lou, Caroline had drawn a blank. Times in the valley were tough, what with record-high gasoline prices and an economic slow-down. Most families she considered as foster parents were farmers, scratching to make ends meet. Even with social services providing support checks for Hannah, taking in another child would cause a financial burden. And those who owned businesses in town were short on time and funds, as well. Ironically, thanks to Eileen's sizable stock portfolio, Caroline herself was the best candidate for fostering Hannah. She had the time and the means. All she lacked was the inclination.

Although lacking inclination wasn't entirely true. Hannah's picture, propped against the sugar bowl, stared at her with big, sad eyes. The child obviously needed lots of love, attention and care. Her father had deserted her, her mother had died, the woman who'd wanted to take her in had also died, and now Caroline was preparing to give her away. Poor kid, shuffled from pillar to post. She probably felt as if nobody cared. And here Caroline was, trying as hard as she could to hand her off to someone else.

But Hannah didn't know Caroline, she assured herself, so surely the little girl wouldn't feel rejected, not if Caroline could find someone who'd give her a loving home. The problem was, who? She stared at the pad with the solitary name at the top, but it provided no answers.

The noise of a vehicle on the cottage road dragged her from her thoughts. She threw down her pencil and strode to the front porch as Ethan's truck came to an abrupt stop in her driveway.

He jumped from the cab and sprinted up the front walk. A man in a hurry, he moved with fluid grace and unmistakable purpose, a sight that took her breath away, even though his hair was mussed and his clothes were covered with dirt. As he came closer, she noted that his face was flushed, and concern filled his hazel eyes.

"You'd better call the police," he said before he reached her.

"What's wrong?"

He mounted the stairs two at a time and stood at arm's length from her, shaking his head, as if in disbelief. "You don't find something like that every day."

"What are you talking about?"

"A body."

Now he had her complete attention. "A body? Where?"

He looked her in the eye, his expression grim. "Buried beneath the compost heap beside the barn at Orchard Cottage. And from the looks of it, it's been there a long time."

Chapter Seven

"Are you sure it's human?" Caroline couldn't believe her ears. "If it's beside the barn, maybe somebody buried a farm animal, like a pig or a cow."

"It's human all right, unless folks around here are accustomed to putting clothes on deceased animals," Ethan said with a grimace.

His answer shook her. Unexplained dead bodies were as rare as hen's teeth in the valley. To know he'd found one on property she now owned was incredible. "You don't have a phone?"

"I have a cell, but it's not an emergency call, so I didn't want to use 911. Do you know the administrative number?"

"It's listed in the phone book." Stunned by his claim, she could only stare at him.

He glared at her with obvious impatience. "Can I borrow your directory, then?"

She snapped into action. "Not necessary. I'll make the call."

Ethan waited on the front porch, refusing to track the dirt that caked his work boots inside. Caroline raced to the phone in the hallway, checked the directory beneath it, and punched in the number of the Pleasant Valley Police Department.

Todd Leland, the dispatcher, answered.

"This is Caroline Tuttle at Blackberry Farm. My new tenant tells me he's unearthed a body at Orchard Cottage."

"Is it human?"

"Yes, and he says it looks as if it's been buried a long time."

Todd informed her that Lucas Rhodes was on patrol nearby and would arrive at her place shortly. "And don't touch anything before he gets there."

With questions buzzing like deer flies in her brain, Caroline returned the handset to its cradle. She didn't know what Ethan had touched or exactly where he'd found the body or even why he'd been digging.

She stepped outside to find him pacing on the front porch. "Lucas Rhodes is on his way."

Ethan raised his eyebrows in question.

"He's a police officer."

"Good." He stopped pacing, leaned against the balustrade, and crossed his arms over his chest. "So we wait."

Even covered in dirt and obviously distraught, he looked handsome. Too handsome for comfort. Caroline relocated to the swing at the other end of the porch and took a seat. "Exactly where did you find this body?"

"On the east side of the barn under the compost heap."

"Under? You were digging *under* the compost pile?"

"I was moving it."

"Why?"

Her question seemed to make him uncomfortable. "It was an eyesore. I'm planning to plant spring bulbs there in the fall. Thought I'd get the ground ready now."

Oh, boy. What was more appealing than a one hundred percent male who planted flowers? She shook off the thought that was bound to lead her into trouble and concentrated on the practical. "It's almost ninety degrees. Why didn't you wait for cooler weather?"

"I don't mind the heat."

Of course not, you idiot. He's a former firefighter, after all.

She pressed her lips together to keep from grinding her teeth. What was it about Ethan that seemed to disengage her brain?

"Who was the last person to live at Orchard Cottage?" he asked.

Caroline thought for a moment. "No one's lived there for more than fifteen years. Eileen used to have a tenant who managed the orchards, but the Mauneys have taken care of the apple crops for years now."

"Do you remember the tenant's name? The police will want to know."

She shook her head. "It's probably in Eileen's

111

records. There's an old secretary in the corner of the parlor filled with ledgers and notebooks. I'll go look."

But before she could enter the house, a cloud of dust lifted near the highway and the sound of tires on gravel announced the arrival of Lucas Rhodes. Within minutes, a black SUV with a light bar on the roof and the shield of the Pleasant Valley Police Department on the doors turned off the road onto the driveway.

Lucas parked beside Ethan's truck, climbed out and came up the walk. Tall with rugged good looks, high cheekbones that suggested a hint of Cherokee ancestry and piercing green eyes, Lucas in his crisply starched dark green uniform was the epitome of the handsome lawman, but his attractive face was grim as he approached. Handsome as he was, Caroline noted that he didn't make her brain go foggy like Ethan did.

She and Ethan descended the porch steps and met Lucas halfway up the farmhouse walk, and Caroline introduced the officer to her tenant.

"What's this about a body?" Lucas fixed his gaze on Ethan and narrowed his eyes with suspicion.

"It's at Orchard Cottage," Caroline said.

Ethan nodded. "I found it while I was digging in the compost heap. *Body* is a misnomer. I guess skeleton is a better word. It's apparently been there a good while."

Lucas keyed the mike of the radio clipped at his shoulder. "I'm at Blackberry Farm and going to check out the unidentified body at Orchard Cottage. Contact the sheriff's crime scene unit and the coroner and have them meet me there."

"Ten-four," Todd's voice sounded from the radio's speaker. "You need any backup?"

"Negative. I'll secure the crime scene and wait for the forensics techs and the coroner."

Lucas turned to Caroline. "Any guess who might be buried there?"

She shook her head.

Lucas keyed his mike again. "Check local missing persons records going back several decades and get me a list of names."

"Ten-four," Todd answered.

"The cottage has been empty a long time. Maybe it was a drifter, a vagrant," Caroline said.

Lucas lifted one corner of his mouth in a lopsided grin. "And he buried himself?"

"Good point." Caroline felt like smacking herself. Ethan's proximity really did have her brain out of commission.

Lucas turned to Ethan. "You're the guy who knows where the body's buried. How about leading the way?"

"Sure. Just follow my truck."

"I'm coming, too," Caroline said.

"You can ride with me," Lucas offered.

She nodded and watched Ethan sprint to his

pickup and hop in. The former firefighter was working a spell on her. The sooner she could leave the valley, the better. She'd waited too many years for her ranch to allow any man, no matter how appealing, to slow her down now.

At Orchard Cottage, Ethan parked in front of the barn and waited for Lucas and Caroline to join him before he rounded the corner and led them to the gaping hole near the bottom of the compost heap.

Lucas surveyed the scene. "Why were you digging here?"

"Clearing the site for planting," Ethan said. "Got tired of looking from the back porch at a mountain of weeds."

Lucas approached the hole, knelt on his haunches and gazed in. Over the cop's shoulder, Ethan could see the bones, stained the color of strong tea, which had brought an abrupt end to his excavation. Even while studying the grisly scene, he experienced a tingle of awareness of Caroline beside him, her quick intake of breath when she spotted the body, the fragrance of her wisteria shampoo mixing with the aroma of rich loam and the scent of honeysuckle growing on a nearby fence.

"Once I recognized the skull and realized these were human remains," Ethan said, "I quit digging. Figured the police would want to do the rest."

"Good thinking," the officer said, not taking his eyes off the darkened bones and scraps of cloth that clung to them.

"Of course," Ethan added, "by then I'd already shifted the majority of the compost to the other side of the barn. Sorry if I've moved any evidence."

"How long do you think it's been there?" Caroline asked.

She seemed perfectly calm, except for the slight tremor in her voice and the pallor of her perfect complexion that emphasized the brilliant sky blue of her eyes. Ethan fought against the impulse to lace his fingers through hers to give her hand a comforting squeeze.

Lucas shrugged and shook his head. "The coroner will have to figure out the time line."

He stood, returned to the SUV and withdrew a roll of yellow tape. With practiced efficiency, he began cordoning off the yard alongside the barn where the compost heap had been, as well as the area where Ethan had moved the dirt to the other side of the barn.

"We'd better get out of his way," Ethan said. "We can watch from the porch."

Caroline followed him up the path he'd trampled through the high grass to the back porch. "Maybe the bones are American Indian," she said. "From the looks of them, they could be hundreds of years old."

"Maybe. But I found them close to the surface, almost as if the body had been left in a shallow trench by the barn and slowly covered with compost to hide its location."

She gave a visible shudder and sank into the nearest chair on the porch. "Are you suggesting he, or she, was murdered?"

Ethan nodded toward Lucas. "Finding that out is his job."

Caroline shook her head. "I can't believe something like that could happen. Not here in the valley."

"Bad things happen everywhere." Ethan slammed his mind shut against horrible memories, recollections he couldn't yet face, much less talk about. "You want some coffee?"

"No, thanks." She kept her gaze focused on the cop who was tying crime tape to the gnarled trunk of an ancient apple tree and asked over her shoulder, "You settling in okay?"

He lowered himself into a chair and propped his feet on the porch balustrade. "It's everything Eileen promised."

Caroline pulled her attention from Lucas and flashed him a smile. "I'm assuming she didn't promise much. You don't even have a phone."

"No problem. Like I said, I have my cell."

She continued to watch Lucas and shook her head. "I'm not sure I'm ready for the responsibilities of landowning."

"I thought that's what you wanted, your own place in Texas. Or was it Montana?"

"I'm leaning toward New Mexico, but that's all temporarily on hold." Her voice was heavy with disappointment, and he wished she wasn't so anxious to leave.

"I don't expect you to honor Eileen's conditions about feeding me." His response was reasonable, but not what he wanted to say. If he had his way, he'd share three meals a day with Caroline for the rest of his life. Before meeting Caroline, he'd never been a believer in love at first sight, but now he considered himself a convert.

"Thanks, but you aren't the holdup. I still have to find a home for Hannah. And I'm running out of time."

"What's the rush? I thought you were going to take your time to sell this place and scope out western locations?"

"I am. But I'm hoping to have a permanent place for Hannah before she arrives Monday. The poor kid's been shifted around enough already. I'd like to spare her an additional move, if I can."

He could read the conflict in her voice. As much as Caroline wanted to move away, she hadn't been immune to the plight of little Hannah. He couldn't have loved Caroline if she had. Any person who could look at the girl's photograph and not be touched didn't have a

117

heart. And Caroline's empathy was only one of the many things about her that attracted him.

"So what are your chances of finding someone by then?"

"I was making a list when you showed up. But so far, it only has one name, and not a very solid prospect at that."

"So it looks like Hannah will be at Blackberry Farm for a while?"

She nodded.

He struggled to suppress his delight. "Need any help getting the kid's room ready?"

She shook her head. "If I can't find another foster family before she arrives, I thought I'd let Hannah pick a new bedspread and curtains for her room."

He remembered Amber when she'd been Hannah's age and how particular she'd been about her bedroom, insisting everything, from the walls to the bedspread, be lavender. "She'll like that. Once she's picked what colors she wants, I'll help you paint."

"Paint?"

"Didn't you want your bedroom walls your own special color when you were a kid?"

Caroline's eyes clouded with memory. "Blue. I had pale blue walls with billowy white draperies and a white bedspread with a ruffled skirt."

"What, no cowboys?"

She shook her head. "That phase came later."

Ethan glanced across the lawn to Lucas's SUV where the cop had retreated after placing the crime tape to wait for the coroner. "What got you so interested in the Wild West? A vacation trip?"

Her blue eyes widened. "How did you know?"

"A lucky guess."

"My parents took me to the Grand Canyon when I was fourteen. I didn't want to go. At that age, all I wanted was to hang out with my friends. But one look at all those wide-open spaces and I was hooked. That and—"

She flushed and shook her head.

"What?" he asked, eager to know what made her tick. "A teenage fascination with Westerns?"

"It sounds silly."

"Try me."

"That summer I also started reading romances set in the West. Later I branched out into all kinds of books with settings in that part of the country."

He nodded with understanding. "Good books have the power to transform lives."

"You're a reader, too?"

"Used to be." The last few months his concentration had been so fractured, he'd found reading anything almost impossible. "I loved a good mystery."

"And now you have a real one in your own backyard."

He grinned, glad to change the subject. "Technically, it's your backyard."

"Maybe you can help me tonight."

"Tonight?" he asked, curious to know what she had in mind but excited by the prospect of spending more time with her.

"After supper." Her expression held no guile, offering nothing more than her words had indicated. "We'll go through Eileen's old ledgers to look for names of everyone who's lived at Orchard Cottage."

He pushed to his feet. "Lucas has everything under control here, and, if there's no ID on the body, the authorities will want those names as soon as possible. Maybe we should start now."

He'd rather Caroline not watch the coroner's removal of the remains. Such a sight could give her nightmares. As an authority on nightmares, he wouldn't wish them on anyone.

He gazed south down the road toward Blackberry Farm. Only the roof of its barn was visible. No other neighbors could be seen from Orchard Cottage. If whoever was buried by the barn had been murdered, the killer had chosen his spot well, isolated and remote.

"A perfect spot to hide a body," Caroline said, as if reading his mind.

"Maybe it was a natural death. If it occurred during the Depression, there would have been no money for a mortuary. Could be the family performed the funeral and the burial."

Caroline shook her head. "Whoever's buried there wasn't loved."

"How do you know?"

"Would you bury someone you care about under a compost heap?"

Talk of burials brought a cascade of memories that threatened to suffocate him. "Let's get started on those ledgers."

Hours later, Caroline shoved a stack of old, yellowed ledgers to one corner of the table and went to the kitchen sink to wash her hands. She'd been enjoying Ethan's company far too much. Since they'd almost completed perusing Eileen's tenant records, the sooner she fed him, the sooner he could leave. And the sooner she could stop thinking about him and return to her list of prospective foster parents for Hannah.

"It's getting late," she said. "I'll fix us some lunch."

Ethan scribbled another name on the pad beside him and closed the ledger he'd been reading. "We've gone all the way back to 1950 and only have a few names."

Caroline dried her hands and hung the towel on a rack by the stove. "Both Orchard Cottage and Meadow Place have been vacant most of that time. Eileen told me that before World War II, Meadow Place, the other house on the property, was rented to a dairy farmer. Most of the young men in Pleasant Valley enlisted during the war. When Meadow Place's tenant went into the navy, his wife sold their herd to Joe Mauney and left the valley to live with her mother. The family didn't return after the war, and Joe still rents Eileen's land."

She rummaged in the refrigerator for sandwich meat, lettuce and condiments, placed them on the counter, and reached into the cabinet for a loaf of bread.

"Eileen's husband was killed?" Ethan asked.

Caroline nodded. "Died in the Pacific right before the war ended. She has his Purple Heart and Bronze Star around here somewhere. According to my mother, Calvin Bickerstaff was a home-town hero."

"And Eileen never remarried?"

"No." Caroline began assembling sandwiches on Blue Willow plates. "Maybe while her husband was overseas, she discovered she liked her solitude."

"Or she could have been a one-man woman," he said. "Loved him so much no other man could measure up. That's how my mom feels about my dad."

Caroline pursed her mouth in thought, then shook her head. "I don't think that's why Eileen remained single. I don't remember her ever talking about him."

"Maybe his death hurt too much to talk about."

She looked up to see the pain in his voice reflected on his face, and her curiosity was aroused. Whom had Ethan lost to cause such misery? Was that loss the reason he'd withdrawn from his life in the busy city of Baltimore to the isolation of Orchard Cottage? Could his grief be the reason he'd expressed such empathy for little Hannah?

Before she could contemplate further, a knock sounded at the front door.

"I'll be right back," she said to Ethan and hurried down the hall to find Lucas, his uniform hat in hand, waiting on the porch.

"You can tell Ethan we're through up at his place," he said.

"They've taken the body?"

Lucas nodded. "The coroner will do an autopsy to see if he can determine cause of death."

"He can tell that, even after all this time?"

"I don't think he'll have a problem." Lucas paused as if reluctant to say more.

"You already suspect something?" Caroline prodded.

Ethan came up the hall and stood beside her. Lucas nodded to him. "Your place is all yours again."

"I can finish moving the compost heap?"

"Have at it," Lucas said. "The forensics techs have sifted all the surrounding dirt."

"We're going through Eileen's records now," Caroline said. "We'll have a complete list of former tenants this afternoon. I'll bring it in to the station."

"Did the techs find any ID on the body?" Ethan asked.

"Some clothing fragments. That's it."

"Any idea how the person died?" Ethan asked.

Lucas hesitated.

"You might as well tell us," Caroline said. "We'll find out eventually."

Lucas took in a deep breath and let it out. "Blunt force trauma. The skull was caved in."

Chapter Eight

By the time Caroline and Ethan had eaten a late lunch and finished going through the ledgers, it was after three o'clock. Ethan headed back to Orchard Cottage, and Caroline grabbed her purse and car keys and climbed into her car for a trip into town.

Driving down the lane toward the highway, she noted that the blackberries growing wild along the meandering split-rail fence would be ripe next week. The sight of the plump berries generated a pang of loss at memories of summer days spent in Eileen's big kitchen, helping her friend make jams and jellies that Eileen, wearing a big straw hat and a broader smile, sold at a roadside stand at the entrance to the farm.

At the highway, Caroline turned left toward town and drove along the road that followed the twists and turns of the Piedmont River on its rush through the valley over rock-strewn beds. Weeping willows lined the riverbanks, their delicate branches in full leaf dipping toward the water. On either side of the river, rolling hills, covered by pastures and corn crops, lifted toward the mountains that surrounded Pleasant Valley like the sides of a bowl. Black-eyed Susans filled the meadows, their cheerful yellow a pleasant contrast to the abundant green of the grasses, trees and distant ridges.

Caroline loved the valley. Leaving it would be hard. It held a special peace and beauty in every season. But as much as she loved the land, its people and the sense of belonging in a place her ancestors had settled three hundred years ago, something was missing. She hoped moving from the only locale she'd ever known would help her find the elusive pieces needed to make her life complete.

She sped past the entrance to Grant and Merrilee's house on the left, then the drive to River Walk on the right. Around the next curve was the veterinary clinic where Grant and his father-in-law, Jim Stratton, cared for the valley's farm animals and family pets.

The highway was so familiar, she could have driven it in her sleep—a good thing, since her concentration was fractured, divided between Ethan Garrison, who'd taken residence in her thoughts with all the persistence of an itch she couldn't scratch, and her overriding concern of finding a family for Hannah.

By the time she reached downtown, Piedmont Avenue, the main thoroughfare, was almost deserted. Area farmers came to town early for their Saturday shopping. Now only a few cars remained in the parking lot at Blalock's Grocery, and Tom Fulton had already placed the "closed" sign in the front door of the department store.

She drove to the far end of Piedmont Avenue, dropped off the list of Eileen's former tenants at the police department, and turned back toward town. The Hair Apparent, down the street from Jodie's café, was closed, too, but Caroline knew where she'd find Amy Lou. She climbed the exterior staircase to the apartment above the beauty shop and knocked on the door.

Amy Lou Baker, still dressed in her pink polyester pantsuit, her standard uniform, opened the door. Her feet, however, were bare. Caroline couldn't remember ever seeing the beautician without her sensible white shoes. The woman still looked exactly as she had when Agnes first brought eight-year-old Caroline to the new shop to have her hair styled. Today, Amy Lou sported the same explosion of teased honey blond hair and a wide, welcoming smile. Only the additional lines in her face attested to the passing years.

"Caroline! I didn't forget an appointment, did I, sugar?"

Caroline shook her head. "I need your help, Amy Lou."

Amy Lou opened the door wide and motioned her inside. Caroline glanced around with interest. She'd never seen Amy Lou's apartment. Like its owner, it was decked out in pink, from the thick shag carpet to the draperies and upholstery. And every surface was covered with knick-knacks and handcrafted items. Amy Lou lifted a crocheted afghan still under construction from the sofa and motioned for Caroline to sit. With a hobbling gait, as if her feet hurt, Amy Lou ambled to a nearby chair, lowered herself with a whoosh of relief, and propped her feet on a footstool.

"How can I help you, sugar? Your mama giving you a hard time about moving?"

"No more than I expected," Caroline said with a rueful smile.

Amy Lou, true to form, was up on all the latest town news. The Hair Apparent served as communications central for Pleasant Valley. Every tidbit of gossip concerning the town and valley either originated or was disseminated within the shop's pale pink walls. Caroline's mother, during her weekly appointment, had probably bent Amy Lou's ears about her ungrateful daughter.

Amy Lou crossed her swollen ankles and pursed her lips. "Then it must be that firefighter from Baltimore."

Caroline shook her head. "He's just a tenant and no problem."

Maybe if she kept saying the words, she'd eventually come to believe them herself and get to a point where she could think of Ethan without her heart beating a little faster. Between inheriting the farm and Hannah, the last thing she needed was a man to further complicate her life.

And where men were concerned, Caroline admitted she was gun-shy. In spite of the happy marriages of her friends, she was well aware that love carried risks and penalties. Look at her mother, so reliant on her husband for everything that her life had fallen apart when he died. As a result of her mother's example, Caroline recognized her hunger for wide-open spaces for what it was: a yearning for independence, freedom and the ability to make her own choices. No man, no matter how perfect, no matter how kind or easy on the eyes, would deter her from those goals. She refused to yield her self-determination to any man, not even a man as attractive and endearing as Ethan Garrison.

"No problem?" Amy Lou was still raving about Ethan. "Sugar, that's not how I heard it. I haven't seen the man myself, but those who have claim he's a problem for every living, breathing female who lays eyes on him. Flat out takes their breath away with those big sad eyes. You're a lucky girl, sharing two meals a day with Mr. Right."

"I'm not looking for Mr. Right."

"Don't need to, do you," she said with a grin, "with him living under your very nose." Her expression sobered. "Where are my manners? Would you like a glass of tea?"

"No, thanks. I'm fine."

Amy Lou sighed and leaned back in her chair. "Probably just as well. After being on my feet all day, I don't know if these old dogs would make it to the kitchen and back. I'm not as young as I used to be."

Amy Lou looked weary, and her usual effervescence had faded. The woman obviously worked too hard. How could Caroline ask her to take on the care of a nine-year-old? On the other hand, maybe Hannah would be a help and comfort to Amy Lou, who'd been widowed for years.

"How come *you're* not looking for Mr. Right?" Caroline asked. "Harold's been gone a long time. Don't you get lonely?"

Amy Lou cocked her head, pursed her lips, and studied Caroline with an intensity that made her want to squirm. "What's on your mind, sugar? I know you're not here to fix me up with a date with your handsome firefighter. Those May-December relationships rarely work."

Caroline smiled. "In your case, it would be more like May-August."

"But that's not why you're here."

Caroline shook her head. "I'm here about Hannah."

"Daniel's little sister? I heard she's coming on Monday. If she's half as nice as that brother of hers, she'll be a sweetheart."

"I'm sure she will be." Encouraged by Amy Lou's attitude, Caroline plunged ahead. "And I'm looking for a foster family for her."

Amy Lou looked surprised. "I thought you were taking her."

Caroline stifled guilty feelings. "I'm selling Blackberry Farm as soon as possible, and I'm hoping to find a permanent place for Hannah before she arrives."

Amy Lou's friendly face reflected her surprise. "And you were thinking *I'd* take her?"

"You're wonderful with people. Especially children. I remember how good you were to me the first time I came to your shop."

"Cutting a child's hair is one thing," Amy Lou said with a shake of her teased and lacquered hairdo. "Raising one up in the way she should go is another thing entirely."

"You'd make a wonderful foster mother."

Amy Lou's bright eyes took on the dreamy look of remembrance. "Harold and I tried to have babies. But it wasn't meant to be. And now, sugar, I'm too old, too tired, too set in my ways. I can hardly drag my weary bones up those stairs at the end of a day. What would I do with an active nine-year-old?"

Disappointment washed through Caroline. Amy Lou had been her best chance of placing Hannah by Monday. "You know everything that goes on in the valley. Can you think of *any* family who would take in Hannah and give her a good home?"

Amy Lou furrowed her brow. "Give me a minute."

"What about Merrilee's parents?"

"Jim and Cat Stratton? They'd make great foster parents." Caroline's surge of hope was short-lived as Amy Lou added, "But they're leaving Monday for a trans-Canada railway trip. A second honeymoon they've been planning since last summer. They'll be gone a month."

Caroline's hope to have Hannah settled in a permanent home on Monday so the child wouldn't have to move again vanished. "Gofer says he's tried everyone. Only Eileen was willing to take Hannah, and now she's passed her on to me."

Amy Lou threaded her fingers together, rested them on her plump midriff, and raised her eyebrows. "You ever stop to think that your having Hannah was meant to be?"

"What's meant to be is that I find a nice little place in New Mexico, out west where I've always wanted to live," Caroline said in frustration.

"You know what they say." Amy Lou's eyes twinkled. "Life is what happens when you're making other plans."

Caroline forced a smile. "Not if I have anything to say about it."

After a late supper that evening, Ethan helped Caroline clear the table. Their meal had been a silent one, with Caroline deep in thought over how to deal with Hannah. The child would arrive on Monday, and Caroline didn't want the little girl to become too attached to Blackberry Farm, since her stay would be only temporary. At the same time, she wanted Hannah to feel welcome, wanted and safe.

How had she managed to land herself in such a conundrum?

"That was terrific spinach lasagna." Ethan's deep voice broke into her thoughts.

She took a moment to orient herself, like someone breaking the surface after a deep dive. "Eileen made it. She left it in the freezer."

Caroline pushed back from the table, took the half-empty casserole dish and covered the left-over pasta with plastic wrap. She placed it in the refrigerator, and Ethan emptied ice from the tea glasses into the sink and put them in the dishwasher. She hadn't asked for his help. He'd simply assumed the tasks, as easily as if they were an old married couple who'd cleaned up together for years. He hadn't complained when she hadn't talked at supper, hadn't tried to force conversation. He'd simply been there, comfortable and

132

easy with the silence. Earlier, she'd been lost in thoughts of Hannah, but now Ethan—with his quiet, helpful manner, his movements, graceful and efficient for such a big man—occupied her mind.

"Mr. Right," Amy Lou had called him. From what Caroline had observed, the title was apt. The man had no obvious faults, unless she counted too agreeable, too helpful, too good-looking in his own rugged way. But also he was too filled with pain from some past trauma that she guessed was related to the burns on his hands and his sabbatical from the fire department.

The more time she spent with him, the more appealing he seemed. Not that he was coming on to her. Any overt moves would have been like a splash of cold water, enough to turn her off to his charms. No, the man was just an all-around nice guy who was inching his way into her life and heart so subtly that if she wasn't careful, one day she'd wake up and wham! She'd be a goner.

How had her life become so complicated in less than a week? She'd lost her friend, inherited a farm, left home for the first time, become a reluctant foster mother, and met a man. She should have been careful what she'd wished for when she was dying of boredom at the B and B.

"Guess where I went this afternoon?" Ethan's smooth voice again shattered her thoughts.

"I give up."

"Archer Farm."

"Did Jeff give you the tour?"

Ethan shook his head and leaned against the counter while she loaded plates in the washer. "I didn't go to see the place. I went to see Daniel."

"Daniel? Were you trying to line up some help with your renovations at Orchard Cottage?"

"No, but that's a good idea. I wanted to talk to him about his sister. He's really glad she'll be living with you."

Caroline wished she shared the teen's enthusiasm. As much as she liked Daniel, as much as she wanted Hannah to have a loving home, she didn't want to be pinned down in the valley.

"How about driving to Walhalla with me tomorrow?" Ethan said suddenly.

"What?"

"There's a Wal-Mart there. It'll have everything we need."

"For what?"

"For Hannah. If we go first thing, we can get back and have her room ready by Monday."

Caroline closed the door to the dishwasher and turned to face him. "I don't know what you're talking about."

"Yellow." Ethan's face glowed with a boyish enthusiasm that only added to his attractiveness.

"What?"

"Hannah's favorite color. Daniel told me. If I buy the paint tomorrow morning, I can paint tomorrow afternoon. I thought you might want to pick out a matching bedspread and some curtains. I'll pay for them," he added quickly.

"You haven't settled into your own place yet. Don't you want to paint there first?"

Now how was she supposed to resist a man so considerate of a little girl's feelings?

"I chose to come to Orchard Cottage." His eyes lost their playfulness and seemed to bore straight through her. "And I'm an adult. Delayed gratification, I believe, is one of the prerequisites of being a grownup. Hannah, however, is a kid who didn't have a choice. Wouldn't it be great to have a beautiful room in her favorite color waiting for her? To let her know you're glad she's here?"

Ethan's compassion made Caroline feel small by comparison. She'd considered Hannah's feelings, trying to find a permanent place so the girl wouldn't have to move again. But had Caroline's efforts been on Hannah's behalf or in her own self-interest?

Ethan was right. Hannah needed to feel welcomed and loved and special, no matter how long or short her stay at Blackberry Farm. If fixing up her room helped, then Caroline was all for it.

"If we leave at eight," she said, "we can be at Wal-Mart before the weekend crowds descend. But, since it's my house, I'll pay for the paint and fabrics. Your offer to paint, however, is gratefully accepted. I always get more paint on me than on whatever I'm painting."

She had her back to the counter with no room to maneuver. Ethan stepped closer and grasped her shoulders lightly. His hazel eyes warmed. She tried, but couldn't look away.

He slowly grasped her hands and pulled her close. "You're a good woman, Caroline Tuttle."

She shook her head. "I'm a selfish woman."

"I don't believe that for a minute. I doubt there's a selfish bone in your body."

She had to keep talking, afraid of what might happen if she stopped, but his proximity was making her dizzy. She grappled for words. "Hannah puts a crimp in my plans."

"If you were selfish, you'd flat out refuse to take her. Eileen knew your heart or she wouldn't have asked you to look after Hannah."

Only a small space separated them. She tried to think of something else—piñon pines and coyotes howling at the moon above the high desert. But her western fantasies evaporated like mist in sunlight next to the reality of Ethan's large, strong hands holding hers.

She shook her head and tried to step back, but the counter blocked her. "I *am* selfish. You're the one who thought of what Hannah needs, not me."

"Not selfish. Just human." He didn't loosen his grip on her hands or break his gaze. "You've dedicated your adult life to your widowed mother, and you were such a good friend to Eileen that she left you everything. Those aren't selfish acts in my book."

"But all I want now is to get away."

His eyes clouded. "From me?"

She started to say yes, but couldn't. Being that close to him felt too good. "From the valley. I want a life of my own."

He wrapped his arms around her and pulled her into a hug. "Why can't you have a life of your own here?" he said softly in her ear.

"Because I'm afraid." The words popped out before she could think. How *could* she think with the thud of his heart against her own?

"Afraid of what?"

"Of being sucked in again by obligations to my mother." She was light-headed from lack of air.

"And?"

He leaned back to face her, and his eyes seemed to look into her soul. But she couldn't look away, and she couldn't lie. "Afraid of losing my independence."

"Independence covers a lot of bases." He held her against him with one arm and traced the line of her cheek with the index finger of his other hand. "Financial, emotional—?"

"Both," she interrupted with a whisper, because she couldn't draw air to speak and couldn't generate the will to push him away.

He smiled, dimples forming in his tanned

cheeks. The green flecks in his hazel eyes sparked. Without warning, he leaned forward, brushed her lips with his—and released her.

She almost stumbled with surprise.

"If it's independence you want," he said in easy agreement, "then I'll do everything I can to help."

"Help?" She was inundated by confusion and longing, while warning bells clamored in her brain.

"Finding a home for Hannah," he said in a matter-of-fact voice. "Getting the farm ready for the market. And once it's sold, I'll even help you pack. How's that?" His expression was open, at ease, friendly. He was apparently willing, even eager, to expedite her departure. Had she only imagined the feelings she'd just seen in his eyes?

She struggled to control her seesawing emotions and think of an appropriate response. Her addled brain refused to cooperate. How could one man, no matter how appealing, send her into total mental meltdown?

He crossed the room, opened the back screen door, then turned to her. "I'll see you a little before eight in the morning. We'll take my truck."

The more distance he placed between them, the quicker her calm would return. "Fine. Eight o'clock."

The screen door slammed and he disappeared.

Good, he's gone, her head insisted. *That was a close call.*

But her heart cried for more of Ethan Garrison.

With the disconnect between her emotions and her brain making her feel out of control, if not out of her mind, Caroline locked the back door and, still wobbly from her close encounter, climbed the stairs to bed.

Chapter Nine

"You missed a spot," Caroline said.

From her vantage point, sitting in the middle of the poster bed in the upstairs bedroom, she pointed to the top of the wall Ethan had just rolled with sunny yellow paint.

"Here?" He swiped the area with the roller.

"That'll do it," she said with a nod.

He stood back and surveyed the newly painted room with satisfaction. "This is better than that faded blue. Much more cheerful."

"And also Hannah's favorite color," Caroline reminded him.

She ripped open a plastic bed-in-a-bag package and removed a yellow gingham dust ruffle, matching pillow shams and a quilted coverlet in a muted pale green-and-yellow plaid. Then she began making up the antique walnut four-poster bed she'd earlier stripped to its mattress. "Too bad this set didn't come with a matching canopy. Maybe I can find some fabric in town and make one."

Ethan was glad his hands were covered with wet paint, which prevented him from reaching for her. Keeping his distance was the hardest thing he'd ever had to do. Last night, he'd needed every ounce of willpower to walk away. But after Caroline had declared she wanted freedom and independence, he'd have been a fool not to give her space.

What he'd really wanted was to kiss her again. The flicker of disappointment he'd noted in her expression when he'd released her had given him hope that, in spite of her desire for emotional independence, she'd wanted another kiss, too. That fleeting discontented look wasn't much, but he wasn't yet ready to admit defeat. He'd take whatever encouragement he could get.

While Caroline made up the bed, Ethan tamped the lid on the paint can and carried the disposable pan and roller downstairs to the garbage can behind the kitchen porch. When he returned to the upstairs bedroom, Caroline was struggling to maneuver a wide two-shelf bookcase into the gable beneath a double window. He moved quickly to help her.

When the bookcase was in place, Caroline stood back and studied it. "It needs a cushion. I'll make one and cover it with the yellow floral fabric I bought today. Then Hannah will have a window seat on top of the bookcase, where she can sit and read and look out across the mountains." She placed her hands on her hips and studied the rest of the room. "And I'll bring in that big wicker chair from the back bedroom and cover its cushions to match the window seat."

Despite her protests about wanting another family for Hannah, Caroline was making every effort to make the little girl feel comfortable and at home.

He shoved his hands into his back pockets to keep from breaking his resolve not to try to hold her again. Somehow, although she hadn't touched a brush or roller, she had a smear of yellow paint on the tip of her chin.

"You're really into this, aren't you?" he asked.

"It's good practice. When I get my own place, I'll redecorate every room."

"And who's going to paint?"

She grinned. "Maybe you could come visit for a week. You're wicked with a paint roller."

"I'm a man of many talents."

"And humble, too," she teased. "I already know you can paint, garden, fight fires and sculpt in metal. What else is in your repertoire?"

"You forgot cooking."

"That's right. You did say you cooked at the firehouse."

"How about I fix supper tonight?"

Her confidence appeared to waver. "At your place?"

"Sure." Why being alone with him at Orchard Cottage made her any more nervous than here at Blackberry Farm, he didn't know, but he could tell from her response that she preferred her home turf. "Or I can cook here while you put the finishing touches on Hannah's room."

She visibly relaxed. "That'll work. Eileen kept the freezer and pantry well stocked. You'll have plenty to chose from."

"Any requests?"

"Surprise me."

He suppressed a grin. A surprise was just what he had in mind.

Caroline placed the vase of daisies on the dressing table and stepped back to admire her handiwork. With its sunny new paint and linens, the previously tired and dull spare bedroom appeared to glow with light, even though the sun had just set behind the mountain ridge visible from the window gable.

The walnut furniture shined with beeswax polish, the crisp gingham curtains, freshly ironed, framed the sparkling clean windows, and the newly made bed was piled with a variety of pillows and a huge white teddy bear with a yellow bow around its neck. She'd filled the bookcase with favorites from her childhood, including several Nancy Drew mysteries, *Black Beauty*, *National Velvet* and *My Friend Flicka*, salvaged from her storage boxes still piled in the living room. Caroline had flipped through the horse stories of her childhood and recognized that her youthful love of the animals had eventually developed into her adult fascination with cowboy culture.

Caroline had also added to the bookcase the entire set of Harry Potter books that Daniel had said his sister had always wanted. The huge bouquet of cheery daisies added the final touch to a space any little girl would love.

The room smelled of beeswax, fresh linens, clear mountain air—and the aroma of something delicious wafting up the stairs. She'd almost forgotten that Ethan was cooking supper.

Caroline washed her hands in the upstairs bathroom, scrubbed paint from her chin, and went downstairs. She turned toward the kitchen, promising herself not to allow a repeat of last night's kiss. After Ethan had left, she'd lain awake for hours, feeling the imprint of her hands in his. In the clear light of morning, she'd recognized the danger—and futility—of those feelings. Tonight, she'd keep her guard up and her heart in lockdown mode.

"I'm out here," Ethan called from the other side of the front screen door.

She stepped into the twilight onto the wide covered porch and blinked in amazement.

Ethan stood behind a chair at a table draped in a white damask cloth, lit by tall tapers and set for two with Eileen's best china and crystal. A nosegay of roses, tied with pink ribbons, lay beside her place.

He pulled out a chair and motioned her toward it. "I said I'd surprise you."

"I meant surprise me with the menu." Feeling awkward and caught off guard but also pleased, Caroline took the seat he offered. She could enjoy a special meal without committing to more, couldn't she?

Ethan sat opposite her. Candlelight accentuated the rugged angles of his face and reflected in his hazel eyes. "Then I hope you're not disappointed in the food."

She directed her attention toward the plates in hopes of calming the rebellious flutter in her heart. Ethan had filled the dishes with braised chicken breasts with mushrooms, fresh French-cut green beans, baby squash and new potatoes.

"It looks and smells wonderful," she said.

"Thanks to Eileen's freezer and abundant garden."

"You work fast."

"I'm glad you think so," he said, smiling.

She ducked her head to cut her chicken and avoid looking at that smile.

She took a bite, chewed and swallowed. "This is delicious. I should ask you to cook more often."

"I don't mind rotating cooking chores."

144

The warm night air swirled around them, and the only light in the gathering darkness emanated from the candles on the table and the evening star ablaze in the cobalt blue of the not-quite-dark western sky.

If he'd hoped to impress her with a romantic meal, his scheme was working. She was falling under his spell, a situation she'd promised herself to avoid. Before she succumbed, she needed a neutral topic to counteract his magic. "Tell me about your sister."

"Amber?" His face crinkled with affection, but just as quickly the light left his eyes. "She's the baby in the family, only eighteen."

"Does she live at home?"

"She does now." His words were simple but his voice rang with sorrow and resignation.

Caroline waited for him to continue, but he didn't. The pain she'd noted so often in Ethan's expression had returned, apparently generated by talk of his family. She changed the subject. "What are your plans for Orchard Cottage?"

He seemed to welcome the switch and replied with enthusiasm. "I want to have the exterior repairs done before cold weather sets in. A few coats of paint. A new roof."

"You'll do the roof yourself?"

"That was my deal with Eileen."

"But it's two stories with a high peak. Isn't that dangerous?"

"I've had plenty of experience with heights and ladders." His expression clouded again.

In frustration, she stabbed a green bean with her fork. Obviously, talking about anything that reminded him of work caused discomfort, too.

He reached for her glass, filled it with iced tea from a nearby pitcher, poured some for himself, and lifted his glass in a toast. "To Hannah's happiness. And to your new frontiers."

She sipped the tea and considered the irony of his words, one wish, for now, canceling the other.

"So," Ethan said, "what are your plans for Hannah?"

This time *she* felt uncomfortable. "I have no idea. I've had no experience with children. Any suggestions will be much appreciated."

"Have her help you."

"Help? I hated chores as a child. I'd rather have been playing. But there's no one for Hannah to play with out here."

He swirled his tea in his glass before taking another sip. "What about berry-picking? She might enjoy that. Fresh air, exercise, sunshine."

Caroline thought for a moment. "The blackberries will be ripe in a few days. I could teach Hannah to make jam and she can help me run the roadside stand like Eileen used to do." She was warming to the idea. "I'd give her the money we make as an allowance. She's probably never had funds of her own."

Ethan grew silent, as if deep in thought, and pushed a piece of squash around his plate. Then he lifted his head and met her gaze straight on. "How about a rodeo?"

Caroline laughed. "Have a rodeo here? We don't even have horses."

He shook his head. "There's a rodeo in Greenville next weekend. Rand gave me four tickets. I thought you, Hannah and Daniel might want to go with me. You do like rodeos?"

"I've never seen one, except on TV."

The harder she tried to resist Ethan's charms, the more he eased his way past her defenses. As much as she loved all things Western, she should turn down his offer and not encourage him. But she couldn't deny Hannah the pleasure of the outing. Or Daniel. The trip to Greenville would be a perfect visit for the siblings, and their presence would provide a good buffer between her and Ethan. Besides, she'd always wanted to see a rodeo.

He had noticed her initial hesitation. "Of course, if you'd rather not—"

"I'd love to," she said quickly. "But I'll have to get permission from Jeff for Daniel to leave Archer Farm. And make sure Hannah's not afraid of crowds or animals. It scares me how little I know about the child."

"You'll do fine. After all, you were a little girl once."

"But my childhood was happy and secure. I didn't live through the traumas Hannah has experienced. And I have no idea how they've affected her. The records that Gofer showed me reveal only that she's shy."

Ethan started to say something but stopped at the sound of a car coming toward the farm on the drive. "You expecting someone?"

Caroline shook her head, placed her napkin on the table and rose from her chair. In the darkness, she could make out only headlights. But when the vehicle stopped and the driver's door swung open, the dome light illuminated Lucas Rhodes.

"Hey, Lucas," she called. "What brings you all the way out here?"

The officer approached the porch, climbed the steps, and stepped into the small circle of candlelight. "Didn't mean to interrupt your meal."

His cocky grin implied he thought he'd interrupted more than eating.

"It's okay," she said, "we were almost finished."

"Any more news on the body?" Ethan asked.

Lucas nodded, his grin vanished, and his face turned grim in the faint light. "That's why I'm here. We got the coroner's initial report."

"And?" Caroline prodded.

"The body is that of a male, late twenties or early thirties."

"Any identification?" Ethan asked.

"Nothing, except a few scraps of clothing,"

Lucas said. "But the clothing included a belt buckle and some collar insignia."

"Insignia?" Caroline said. "What kind of insignia?"

"A soldier's," Lucas replied, "and what we found on the body is vintage World War II."

Chapter Ten

Ethan had welcomed Lucas's unexpected arrival. His attack of uneasiness, evoked by Caroline's innocent questions about his sister and his own reference to ladders, had dashed his high hopes that a romantic dinner would impress Caroline.

It wasn't Caroline's fault, however, that he couldn't think of Amber without seeing the tears in his sister's eyes or remembering how she'd quit her freshman year of college to stay home with their grieving mother. And he couldn't think of his former job, much less talk about it, without experiencing a choking anxiety, tightness in his chest and a bad case of the shakes. Going to pieces over a simple conversation wasn't the way to win Caroline's heart. More likely he'd send her running in the opposite direction. He was lucky she hadn't turned him down flat on the rodeo.

"You think the body's been buried at Orchard Cottage since World War II?" Caroline was asking Lucas.

"It's possible," the officer said. "All we know for sure at this point is that he was male, a big man, about six feet five inches tall, and probably weighed over two hundred pounds."

"That is a big guy," Ethan observed.

"Probably took another big guy to do him in," Lucas added. "Cause of death was definitely the blunt force trauma that caved in the back of his skull."

"The back?" Caroline asked. "Then someone could have sneaked up on him from behind?"

Ethan thought for a moment. "What if the man wasn't a soldier? Or from WWII? What if he was a vagrant, dressed in army surplus?"

"It's not out of the question," Lucas said. "There have been lots of military surplus stores around since World War II that sell vintage uniforms."

"He could have been working on the barn roof," Ethan speculated. "Looks as if it hasn't been repaired in decades. Maybe he slipped, fell and hit the back of his head, killing him."

"Then why wasn't it reported?" Caroline asked. "And why was he buried in the compost pile? Eileen was one of the most decent women I've ever known. If she was aware of the death, she'd never have condoned burying the man without proper respect, even if he'd been a vagrant."

Lucas took off his uniform hat and scratched his head. "We ran the list of former tenants against

150

every missing persons data bank available. No matches."

"What about matching DNA?" Caroline asked.

"If the body is World War II era—and the coroner believes it's been buried that long—the DNA's not in any data bank," Lucas said.

"Dental records?" Ethan asked.

"Same problem," Lucas admitted.

"So we may never know who he was," Caroline said.

"That's why I'm here," Lucas said. "Have you gone through all of Eileen's records?"

Caroline shook her head. "We've been getting the room ready for Hannah's arrival tomorrow."

"Daniel's sister?" Lucas said.

Caroline nodded.

Ethan still hadn't become accustomed to how everyone always knew everything about everyone else's business in the valley. The whole town apparently was aware of Hannah's impending arrival and her relationship to Daniel at Archer Farm.

"So you're going to have your hands full," Lucas said to Caroline with a sympathetic look.

"Afraid so," Caroline replied. "But not too busy to help you out. Eileen has volumes of diaries, going back to her arrival at Blackberry Farm as a bride. I'll start reading through them after Hannah's in bed at night. If they give any clues to who was buried at Orchard Cottage, I'll let you know."

Lucas nodded. "I'd appreciate it. Whoever it is may have family somewhere, still wondering where he is and what happened to him. It'd be good to give them some peace of mind."

"I'll see what I can find," Caroline said. "Thanks for coming all this way to fill us in."

"No problem. I was patrolling Valley Road anyway."

"Want a cup of coffee and a piece of pie?" Ethan asked. "We were just about to have dessert."

Lucas glanced at the table set for two, then back to Ethan with the look of a conspirator. "Thanks, but I should get on the road."

He donned his hat and headed back to his car.

"How about you?" Ethan asked Caroline. "Want dessert? One of Eileen's cobblers from the freezer is in the oven. It should be done about now."

Her smile seemed too bright, almost forced. "As long as there's ice cream to go with it. Want some help?"

"No, thanks. I'll be right back."

Whatever illusion of romance Ethan had managed to create earlier, Lucas's visit had shattered. Nothing like talk of dead bodies to spoil a mood.

But there would be other nights, Ethan assured himself. And if he could conquer his nightmares and enlist Hannah as an ally, maybe the two of them could persuade Caroline to forget her Wild West fantasy and stay in the valley.

. . .

The next morning, Caroline paced the front porch and watched the road for signs of a car. Gofer and a worker from social services would be arriving soon with Hannah. The little girl's room was completed, Caroline had stocked the kitchen with foods she hoped the child would like, including a supply of SpaghettiOs and Cheerios—and everything was ready.

Except Caroline.

When it came to caring for children, she was flying by the seat of her pants. With no siblings and too many years since she'd been a child, she felt woefully unprepared to relate to a nine-year-old. She didn't know the latest toys, the most popular kids' television shows or little girls' fashions. She'd read the Harry Potter books, but envisioned only a handful of conversations about wizards and Muggles before running out of conversation topics.

Most of all, she worried about Hannah. She couldn't begin to imagine what the girl had suffered, living with an alcoholic mother, then orphaned so young. How could she heal the holes in Hannah's heart? And what right did she have to try when she'd be handing the girl over to another family as soon as possible?

She should have spent last night searching the Internet for information on child-rearing. But her fizzled dinner conversation with Ethan had left her too unsettled and restless to confront the issue. After he'd left, to drive his image from her mind, she'd sat for hours at the computer in Eileen's living room, ordering books on horses and cattle ranching and researching real estate Web sites in western states.

In a flash of luck, she'd discovered a listing for forty-two acres outside Taos, New Mexico. At $175,000, the property—with a dilapidated barn and a small adobe house in worse shape than the barn but with panoramic mountain views—was just what she was looking for. The sale of Eileen's property should bring Caroline enough to buy the property in the Land of Enchantment and leave enough for repairs on the house and barn, as well as money for livestock, including a good saddle horse. As soon as she had Hannah settled, she would approach the bank for a loan, using Blackberry Farm as collateral, and make an offer on the Taos ranch. With Hannah and Ethan pushed from her mind, Caroline had gone to bed and dreamed of New Mexico.

The purring of an engine brought her back to the present, but the sound didn't originate on the highway. Ethan's pickup was coming down the dirt road from Orchard Cottage. Maybe he was headed into town to the builders' supply or hardware store.

He'd seemed strangely subdued once Lucas had left last night. After they'd finished dessert, he'd

154

insisted on doing the dishes alone, then had left with barely a word. She hadn't known whether she'd been relieved or disappointed. A part of her had longed for another kiss, but her practical side had insisted that involvement with Ethan was a waste of time, since, once she left the valley, she'd probably never see or hear from him again. And emotional ties to any man, even one as attractive as Ethan, didn't fit into her plans.

Her practical nature, however, couldn't stop the flicker in her pulse when, instead of continuing toward the highway, Ethan parked in front of the farmhouse. When he climbed out of the cab and strolled toward her up the walk, he was a different person from the morose, brooding man who'd left the night before. His smile, as wide and bright as a summer sunrise, kicked up the speed of her heartbeat.

"Thought you might like some moral support with your new arrival," he said when he reached the porch. He smelled of soap and clothes fresh from the line. "If the conversation lags between you and Hannah, we can always talk to each other."

The more she tried to resist him, the better he was at being irresistible, as well as coming up with ways to make her feel good.

"What are you," she said, "a mind reader?"

He shrugged. "I thought how I'd feel with an unfamiliar child on my hands."

"If you're the cavalry, you arrived just in time." Her stomach clenched with nervousness as a dark, official-looking sedan drove up the drive from the highway and pulled in next to Ethan's truck.

A middle-aged woman with nondescript features and brown hair and dressed in a navy blue pants suit stepped out from behind the wheel. Gofer exited the passenger door. After a wave to Caroline, he opened the rear door, and a tiny girl scooted off the rear seat and onto the drive.

Caroline had steeled herself to remain emotionally detached from Hannah, but one look at the little waif shattered her original intentions. Too small for her age and with pathetically thin arms and legs, Hannah was dressed in threadbare shorts, a faded T-shirt and tattered sneakers. And the child had the worst haircut Caroline had ever seen. The red curls from her photograph had been cropped close to her head in uneven clumps, as if sawed with dull scissors. Looking like a refugee, Hannah glanced at her surroundings, but her wide, blue eyes held a haunted expression, as if she expected the worst from life and had never been disappointed.

"Look at those eyes," Ethan whispered. "That's an old soul if I ever saw one."

Drawn to Hannah in a way she'd never anticipated, Caroline hurried down the walk toward the child. She knelt and held out her arms. "I'm

156

Caroline Tuttle. Welcome to Blackberry Farm."

The little girl approached but stopped a few feet away and ignored Caroline's outstretched arms.

"It's very pretty," she said in a voice that sounded grown-up, despite its childish timbre. "Daniel said it would be."

Hannah's words were complimentary but had lacked emotion, as if the child was numb to the world. Caroline dropped her arms to her sides. Hannah apparently didn't want to be touched.

"I'm glad you like it." The little girl's shell-shocked demeanor made Caroline want to cry. She blinked away tears. "I hope you'll like your room, too. We fixed it up special for you."

"You did?" Hannah seemed surprised, as if no one had ever done something just for her.

Ethan joined them on the walk, but Gofer and the social worker hung back, as if to allow Hannah the opportunity to meet Caroline and adjust to her new surroundings.

"This is Ethan," Caroline said to the girl. "He lives up the road, and he gave your room a new coat of paint."

"Yellow," Ethan said. "Daniel told us it's your favorite color."

Hannah nodded solemnly. "Yes, it is. Thank you."

The child's manners were impeccable, and Daniel's reputation for politeness was well-known throughout the valley. Somehow, despite alcoholism and single-parent status, Hannah's mother had instilled social graces in both her children.

Behind Hannah, the social worker shifted from one low-heeled pump to the other, a visible sign of her impatience to finish her paperwork and be gone.

"Why don't you let Ethan show you around?" Caroline said to Hannah.

Ethan held out his hand. After a moment's hesitation and an encouraging nod from Caroline, Hannah placed her small hand in his and walked beside him toward the backyard and the barn.

"Do you have any animals here?" Caroline heard Hannah ask.

"Not anymore," Ethan told her. "There used to be cows and chickens."

Hannah sighed so heavily, Caroline could hear, even at a distance. "I wish there were horses. I really like horses."

Caroline smiled. She and Hannah had something in common after all.

The pair disappeared around the side of the house, and Gofer spoke at Caroline's elbow. "What do you think?"

"She breaks my heart."

Gofer introduced the social worker. "This is Catherine Benson."

All business, Ms. Benson pulled a sheaf of papers from her briefcase. "I'll need your signature on these."

"We can use the table on the porch." Caroline

led them up the walk and onto the porch, where Ms. Benson spread papers on the wicker table and handed Caroline a pen. "Sign where I've marked with a yellow highlighter, please."

Feeling as if she were jumping off a cliff, Caroline skimmed the contents, then placed her signature on the designated lines and returned the papers to the social worker.

"Is that all?" Caroline asked.

"For now." Ms. Benson stuffed the papers into her briefcase. "I'll stop by in a week or two to see how Hannah is settling in."

With a nod, she turned, descended the stairs, and headed for her car.

"Call me if you need me," Gofer said. "I'll bring Daniel over tomorrow to see his sister."

He turned to leave, but Caroline stopped him. "Have you had any luck finding another foster family?"

Gofer raised his eyebrows. "You've seen Hannah, and you still don't want to keep her?"

"She needs a real family, one with a mother and father and stability, not me."

Gofer cocked his head and fixed her with a stare. "You might be surprised to find that you're exactly what Hannah needs."

"You've talked to her," Caroline protested. "The child is far too old for her years. She doesn't laugh or smile. I haven't the vaguest idea how to fix that."

"Just love her."

"But—"

Ms. Benson's impatient honking of the car's horn interrupted Caroline's protest.

"Gotta go," Gofer said. "Good luck."

"Thanks. I'll need it."

Caroline watched Gofer climb into the sedan. When the car drove away, she hefted the small backpack with Hannah's belongings that Gofer had given her and went in search of Ethan and Hannah. She met them at the steps to the back porch.

"Are you hungry?" Caroline asked. "I have milk and cookies."

"No, thank you," Hannah said.

Caroline had never known a child to turn down cookies—unless she was ill. "Are you feeling all right?"

Hannah gazed up at her with sad eyes. "I miss my mommy."

"Of course you do, sweetie." Caroline cast a what-do-I-do-now look at Ethan.

"Ready to see your new room?" he asked Hannah.

"Okay."

Hannah's response was automatic and without enthusiasm. Caroline feared if someone asked the child to jump off a bridge, her response would be the same numb cooperation.

"You take Hannah upstairs," Ethan said. "I need to get something out of my truck."

Panicked at being alone with the child, Caroline watched Ethan sprint through the yard to the front of the house. With a deep breath, she offered Hannah her hand. "Your room's upstairs, just across the hall from mine."

Hannah placed her hand in Caroline's, and, in spite of the growing heat of the summer day, the girl's fingers felt like ice. She was probably scared to death. Caroline knelt and wrapped her arms around Hannah's stiff, unyielding body. "It's going to be all right, sweetie. You'll see."

Hannah didn't move, didn't speak.

Frustrated at her inability to break through the child's frozen demeanor, Caroline pushed to her feet and grasped Hannah's hand again. "Come with me."

Hannah tagged along obediently, passing through the dining room and entry hall with barely a glance at her surroundings. The soles of her raggedy tennis shoes squeaked as she climbed the stairs beside Caroline. In the upstairs hall, Caroline moved ahead of her to the front room and flung open the door with a flourish.

"Well, what do you think?"

She hadn't expected a squeal of delight but was disappointed when the sunny room didn't elicit even a smile.

"It's very nice, thank you." Hannah said.

"It's all yours," Caroline said. "You can arrange it any way you like."

Hannah glanced around, taking in the book-filled case beneath the window seat, the cheerful yellow walls, and the white teddy bear propped against the pillows.

Hoping for a response, any response, Caroline prodded, "Do you like it?"

Hannah lifted her sorrowful gaze. "It's a very big house."

Caroline felt helpless. Hannah was grieving and frightened, and Caroline didn't have a clue how to help her.

"It is a big house," she agreed, "but I'll always be here with you, so you'll never be alone. And tomorrow Daniel will come to visit."

"Really?" A hint of a smile lighted her eyes, then was gone. "Promise?"

"I promise." And if, for any reason, Daniel didn't come, she and Hannah would track him down. Caroline would do whatever it took to bring the light back to those big, sad eyes.

Boots clamored up the stairs, and Ethan appeared in the doorway, bearing a huge package covered with bubble wrap and tied with a big yellow ribbon.

"This is for you," he told Hannah.

The girl took a step back. "What is it?"

"It's a welcome-to-Blackberry-Farm present. Want to open it?"

He set the package on the window seat, and Hannah approached it with caution. She glanced at it, then back at Ethan, who encouraged her with a nod. "Just untie the bow, and you'll see what it is."

Hannah reached out tentatively and pulled one end of the yellow ribbon. The bow unfastened and the bubble wrap fell away to reveal a basket filled with items. Hannah looked at the contents, then turned back to Ethan with a puzzled frown. "What are they?"

"Bubbles," Ethan said with a smile. "All kinds."

Caroline could have hugged him. Apparently when he'd wandered off while she'd been shopping for bed linens yesterday, he'd purchased the items to assemble into Hannah's gift basket.

Ethan stepped forward and picked up a large pink bottle from the basket. "This is bubble bath. There's a big ole bathtub down the hall that's perfect for bubble baths."

Hannah nodded.

Ethan selected another item. "And these are bubble toys, ducks to play with in the bubble bath."

"I'm too old for toys," Hannah said.

"Then can I have them?" Ethan said. "I'd love to play with them in my bathtub."

"You?" Hannah shook her head. "You're too old, too."

"You're never too old to have fun, kid. How about this?" He selected a box covered in shrink-wrap. "Bubble gum. We can have a contest, you,

163

Caroline and I. We'll see who can blow the biggest bubble."

Hannah looked skeptical, and Ethan set the gum aside. "But first, here's the best. It's a bubble shooter. You fill this end with the bubble liquid, here, pull the trigger and . . ."

Dozens of bubbles erupted from the mouth of the toy and floated like jewels in the morning sunshine streaming through the windows.

Hannah watched the bubbles swirl in the air, but her face never lost its solemn appearance. Ethan, however, did not seem deterred. He dug again into the basket, pulled out an opaque plastic bubble, and handed it to Hannah. "You can open this one."

Without enthusiasm, Hannah twisted the bubble to unscrew its halves. Inside the sphere lay a delicate bracelet, a chain of enameled daisies.

"Daniel told me you like daisies," Ethan said.

"Want me to put it on you?" Caroline asked.

"Yes, please." Hannah stuck out her stick-thin arm.

Caroline placed the bracelet around the girl's wrist and fastened the clasp. "It looks very nice."

"Now this one." Ethan handed Hannah another sphere that opened to reveal a matching necklace.

Caroline put the necklace around Hannah's tiny neck and secured the clasp. "You look very stylish."

"Thank you."

Caroline wanted to scream with frustration.

Ethan had done everything but tap-dance, yet nothing seemed to touch Hannah, who seemed to be frozen in a block of ice. Caroline yearned to see the child laugh. Even a smile would be a start. Hannah's unhappiness tore at her heart.

"So much for the presents." Ethan moved the basket from the window seat and sat down. "Now for the fun part."

He patted the cushion beside him. Hannah looked to Caroline, as if for permission.

"It's okay," Caroline said.

Hannah hopped onto the seat beside Ethan, who'd grabbed the large sheet of bubble wrap that had covered the basket. He spread the wrap across their laps.

"Okay," he said. "Here's the deal. You start on your side, and I'll start on mine. Whoever pops all the bubbles to reach the middle first wins . . ." He paused, as if thinking.

"Wins what?" Hannah asked.

Ethan looked at Caroline. "A trip to the rodeo."

Hannah caught her breath. "A real rodeo? With horses?"

Ethan nodded. "The real deal. Ready. Set. Go."

He paused to let Hannah pop the first bubble. It exploded with a bang that startled her, but she bent her head to her task and moved to the next bubble. By the time she'd worked a quarter of the way through the wrap, Hannah, miracle of miracles, was smiling.

Ethan slowed his progress and lifted his head to meet Caroline's gaze.

Caroline tried to look away, but she was a goner. How could she not care for a man who had worked so hard to make a little girl smile?

Chapter Eleven

"You win!" Ethan shouted when Hannah had popped the bubbles in the wrap all the way to the middle. "Next weekend, little lady, you're going to the rodeo in Greenville!"

Hannah looked stunned. "Can Daniel come, too?"

"An excellent idea," Ethan said with a wink at Caroline.

"But how will we get there?" Hannah asked.

Ethan pretended to think for a minute. "Maybe Caroline and I can take you in my truck."

Hannah nodded, and some of the stiffness eased from her body. "Thank you."

"You're welcome," Ethan said. "Now, how about I fix lunch while Caroline helps you unpack?"

Ethan was marvelous with children, Caroline thought. His sister must adore him. Caroline was finding him much too adorable herself.

"You like peanut butter and jelly?" Ethan asked Hannah.

"Yes, please."

He pushed to his feet. "PB&J, coming right up."

"We'll be down in a few minutes," Caroline said.

After Ethan left, Caroline turned to Hannah. "Let's unpack your backpack."

Hannah slid from the window seat and went to the backpack Caroline had placed on the bed. Hannah unzipped it and removed a small stack of clothes—jeans, a pair of shorts, two more T-shirts and a nightgown. The clothes, like the ones she wore, were faded and worn, looking like thrift store rejects. The child didn't even own a second pair of shoes.

Caroline opened the bottom drawer of the bureau and placed the clothes inside. They didn't fill the space.

"I know what we'll do after lunch," Caroline said.

Hannah looked at her, but said nothing.

"We'll go shopping. Do you like to shop?"

Hannah shrugged. "I don't know. We never went shopping, except sometimes to the grocery store."

"We'll go to Fulton's Department Store, buy you some new clothes, then stop for ice cream at Paulie's Drug Store."

"Okay." But the reply came without enthusiasm.

Caroline placed her hand on Hannah's badly shorn head. "Who cut your hair, sweetie?"

"I did. I tried to cut it all off, but the scissors weren't very good."

"Why did you want it all off?"

"Because the other kids tease me and call me names, like carrottop."

"When I was your age, one of my best friends had hair your color."

"Did the kids tease her, too?"

Caroline nodded.

"Did she cry?"

Caroline thought of Brynn at Caroline's age, but such a different child, infused with feisty self-confidence, even though she, too, had lost her mother. But Brynn had a father who'd worshipped his little girl. Hannah had no one, except an absent brother. "No, she didn't cry. She laughed at them and told them they were just jealous."

"Jealous?"

"Because they all had plain old blond or brown hair while hers was the color of new pennies."

"Really?"

"Really. Brynn has beautiful hair—just like yours."

Hannah looked doubtful, making Caroline all the more anxious to connect emotionally with her and somehow bolster the child's self-esteem.

Maybe Caroline could get Amy Lou to even up Hannah's haircut while they were in town this afternoon. And Amy Lou would get a chance to meet Hannah and perhaps change her mind about fostering the child.

· · ·

That evening, Ethan put the last of the supper dishes in the dishwasher, added detergent and started the wash cycle. Upstairs, Caroline was getting Hannah ready for bed. He'd knocked himself out trying to elicit more smiles from the kid during the meal, but she'd remained her solemn, stoic little self. Just watching her tore at his heart and made him grateful for his parents, his siblings and his normal, fun-filled childhood. Jerry was gone, but the years of life his brother had enjoyed had been happy ones. Ethan couldn't remember when Jerry hadn't been grinning or laughing, telling jokes and playing pranks, alive and loving it. Poor little Hannah acted as if life was one big funeral and she was the principal mourner.

What he wouldn't give to coax a belly laugh out of her.

At the sound of footsteps in the upstairs hall, he moved into the front parlor to wait for Caroline. She descended the stairs, and when she saw him, made a quick swipe at her eyes. But not before he glimpsed tears.

"She's asleep," she said. "I think our shopping trip wore her out."

"That and the trauma of coming to live with strangers." He plopped onto the sofa and patted the cushion beside him. "Bad enough the kid's lost her mother. Now she's lost everything that's familiar, too."

"But her former life must have been so grim." Caroline sat beside him. "Her clothes were little more than rags, and it's obvious she's never had enough to eat. In spite of that, she barely touched her supper."

"Give her time. She needs to adjust."

"I haven't had a chance to tell you how great your bubble basket was."

"I felt as if I struck out on that one. The kid's obviously not into bubbles."

"But at least you tried."

"I remember how Amber used to love surprise presents when she was a kid, especially silly stuff. Hannah's not into silly. She was probably born an adult."

Caroline leaned back and pushed her fingers through her hair. "I feel so guilty."

"About what?" Her wisteria scent threatened his concentration.

"About the fact that Hannah will no sooner become accustomed to this place before she'll be moved to another home." She turned to face him. "You should have seen her. She went through the motions of her bath, in spite of the bubbles, and getting ready for bed like a sleep-walker. The poor kid's shell-shocked. She needs love and stability and joy in her life."

"You can give her all that. I'll do what I can to help."

"I can't give her anything if I'm not here."

"No." He hoped her thoughts were headed in the same direction as his.

Caroline leaned her head against the cushion and stared at the ceiling. "I did a lot of thinking this afternoon."

"And?" He held his breath.

"Watching Hannah, seeing how needy she is, I realize how truly selfish I am."

"Thought we'd already covered the selfish angle and discounted it."

She shook her head. "Only in theory. It takes on a whole other dimension when I'm with Hannah and see how unhappy she is. In light of that, what difference will another year make in fulfilling my dream?"

"You tell me."

"I'm an adult who, as you said, should be used to delayed gratification. But Hannah needs so much, someone who's always there for her with love and attention. And she needs it *now*."

He sat very still, digesting her words. "Are you saying you won't be leaving soon?"

Caroline bolted upright. "How can I? I'd be the worst kind of monster to abandon a little girl who needs me."

I need you, too, he wanted to say, but didn't. "What about your dreams?"

"New Mexico will still be there in a year."

He needed every ounce of muscle control to keep from leaping from the couch and punching his fist in the air in celebration. He'd known Caroline couldn't abandon Hannah. She was too innately good.

"But what happens to Hannah at the end of the year?" he asked. "If she grows to love you and you leave, won't you be placing her in a situation similar to what she faces now?"

Caroline's bright eyes dimmed. "I'll have to find a new family for her in plenty of time for her to make a transition before I leave. In the meantime, she'll be close to Daniel, and I can give her my undivided attention and care."

"Maybe you'll take her to New Mexico with you." He hated to think of Caroline going away, but her amended schedule gave him time to plead his case. If things worked out the way he hoped, maybe she'd take him to New Mexico, too.

A ready-made family. The prospect pleased him.

Caroline shook her head. "It's too soon to plan. I'll just have to wait and see what develops. Maybe Cat and Jim Stratton will agree to take Hannah in a year when I get ready to leave. Cat's a teacher and wonderful with children. And Jim's a vet who could provide her with exposure to the horses she loves. Hannah would be happy there."

Ethan reached for her hand and twined his fingers with hers. "What's important is that you'll be here now, when Hannah needs you."

"What if I'm not enough? What if I can't melt that icy shell she's encased in?"

"Don't borrow trouble." With his other hand, he hooked a blond curl behind her ear and caressed her cheek. "Hannah hasn't been here a full day yet. She needs time to adjust, to trust you."

"What's trust got to do with it?" She leaned into the palm of his hand.

"Everyone has walked out on this kid in one way or another. Her father, her mother. Even Daniel, when he got into trouble. She needs to trust that you'll be here for her."

Caroline jerked away, stood, and paced in the middle of the room. "But I won't. Not if I'm leaving in a year, once Daniel finishes high school. Hannah will just add me to the list of people who've deserted her."

He pushed to his feet, went to her, and wrapped his arms around her. "It will work out. One way or another."

She leaned back in his arms and stared at him, as if searching his face for answers. "How can you be so sure?"

"You have to have faith that events happen for a reason. That there's a purpose, especially for the people who come and go in our lives."

Her scrutiny deepened. "You really believe that?"

"I do."

To his surprise, he felt a shift in his heart, a hairline crack in the hard shell that had imprisoned him since Jerry's death. The pain wasn't gone, but it was different, not as all-consuming and relentless as it had been. And in place of the agony flowed an emotion so powerful, it took his breath.

Forgetting his promise to himself to take things slow, he bent his head and claimed her lips. She stiffened at first, then melted against him. He could feel the thud of her heartbeat as she lifted her arms to the back of his neck. A happiness he hadn't experienced in a long, long time flooded through him.

Suddenly she jerked away and cocked her head. "Listen."

With reluctance, he released her and heard what had captured her attention. In the stillness of the old house, small sobs sounded in the upstairs bedroom.

"It's Hannah," Caroline said. "She's awake. And it sounds like she's crying her eyes out. I should go to her."

Caroline broke from his embrace, crossed the room and hurried up the stairs. Concerned for Hannah, Ethan followed.

He entered Hannah's room as Caroline climbed beside the little girl on the big bed, put her arms around the sobbing child, and stroked her hair. The only illumination came from a daisy-shaped night light and moonbeams filtering through the curtains, but Ethan could see well enough to make out the streaks of tears on Hannah's face.

"Shhh," Caroline whispered to the child. "It's

all right. I'm here, and I'll stay with you tonight."

"I'm here, too." Ethan settled into the wicker chair beside the bed.

Caroline held Hannah, crooned lullabies, and rocked her. Ethan stretched his legs in front of him, determined to remain until the child fell asleep. Eventually, the only sounds were the ticking and occasional chime of the grandfather clock in the downstairs hall, the rustle of wind in the maples outside the open window, and Caroline's soft, even breathing, synchronized with Hannah's.

Ethan waited until he was certain both Hannah and Caroline were asleep. Then he took a quilt from the foot of the bed, tucked it around Caroline, kissed her forehead, and left the room.

He eased down the stairs and out the front door to keep from waking them, and, although he was headed to his lonely room at Orchard Cottage, his spirits lifted with an emotion he hadn't experienced in a long time.

Hope.

Chapter Twelve

Caroline pulled off her broad-brimmed straw hat, wiped berry-stained fingers on her cutoff jeans, and called to Hannah a few feet down the drive from the entrance to the farmhouse. "Ready for a break? I have lemonade in the cooler."

"Okay." Hannah dropped the blackberry she had just plucked into the galvanized pail at her feet, picked up the bucket, and brought it to Caroline.

Caroline peeked inside the pail where berries barely covered the bottom. With Hannah using only thumb and forefinger and selecting each berry with the precision of a quality control inspector, the girl might pick all day and not fill the bucket. But lack of production wasn't Caroline's concern.

"Are you having fun, sweetie?"

"Yes . . . but not as much fun as the rodeo last week." Hannah turned her face upward and met Caroline's gaze with her customary solemn expression. "I really liked the horses."

"I did, too." Wanting to hug the child but knowing from experience that she'd resist, Caroline instead took a can of lemonade from the ice in the cooler, popped the top and handed it to Hannah. "Some day, I'd like to have a horse."

Hannah's expression brightened to almost a smile. "Will you let me ride it?"

Caroline hesitated. She hadn't broached the subject of her eventual move with Hannah. The girl had been settling in so well the past two weeks, Caroline didn't want anything to cast a pall on the child's adjustment.

"Give her a routine she can count on," Gofer had recommended the afternoon he'd brought Daniel to visit his sister. "It will make her feel secure."

So Caroline had concentrated on establishing a pattern—regular bedtimes and risings, minor chores and a little television and reading a chapter from a favorite book before bed each night—except Saturday, when they stayed up later to watch Disney videos and eat popcorn.

Ethan had surprised her by wanting to watch movies with them, and Caroline had been glad of his presence. He had a unique ability to relate to Hannah, while Caroline was still feeling her way. Hannah obviously enjoyed Ethan and his teasing, and although she still hadn't laughed—except an almost-chuckle at the rodeo clowns last Friday—Ethan with a funny face or silly joke could occa-sionally coax her to smile.

Last night at supper, as they'd gathered around the big pine table in the kitchen for fried chicken and fresh vegetables from the garden, their resemblance to a real family had struck Caroline. Ethan had discussed the progress of his repairs on Orchard Cottage, Hannah had told him about learning to make jelly, and Caroline had marveled at the turn her life had taken in such a short space of time.

Except for a quick peck on the cheek whenever he arrived or left, Ethan hadn't kissed her since the night of Hannah's arrival. But Caroline knew he wanted to—and she felt the same way. She just hoped her own expression didn't give her away. She wanted his arms around her as much as he did, but she resisted, shoving the thought into a corner of her mind and locking the door. When the time came to leave the valley, saying goodbye to Hannah would be hard enough. Caroline didn't want the extra complication of pining for Ethan or to have her independence fettered by an infatuation with no future. If she wasn't careful, the tender snare of love for the little girl and bonds of attraction for Ethan would trap her in the valley more firmly than any obligations to her mother ever had.

"It's all right." Hannah's voice broke into her thoughts.

"What?"

"You don't have to let me ride your horse if you don't want to. It was rude of me to ask."

"Oh, Hannah. Of course I'll let you ride my horse. I was just thinking how long a time it will be before I get one."

Hannah swigged lemonade from the can and cast Caroline a worried look. "I haven't helped very much, have I?"

"What?"

The child nodded toward her pail. "I'm not very good at picking blackberries."

"It's not a contest, sweetie. You do it because it's fun. Fresh air, sunshine, a gorgeous summer day. And all the blackberries you can eat."

"I can eat them?"

Caroline noted the girl's lips were clean without

a trace of berry stain anywhere, except her fingers. "Of course you can. Do you like them?"

Hannah shrugged. "I never ate a blackberry."

"Close your eyes and open your mouth."

As always, Hannah did exactly as she was told. With her fragile bones, delicate build and open mouth, she reminded Caroline of a needy baby bird. Caroline selected the plumpest berry from her own pail and popped it into Hannah's mouth.

"Now chew," Caroline instructed.

She half expected Hannah to spit it out, but her lips closed on the berry and her eyes flew open in surprise. "It's good."

"You betcha. And you can eat as many as you want."

"But what about our jelly?"

Caroline waved her arm at the brambles lining the fence. "We have more berries than we can ever pick. We'll have plenty for jelly."

"When will you open the stand?"

"In a few days, as soon as we make jelly from this batch. And as I promised, you can keep all the money we make."

"Thank you."

"What will you buy? More books? Some clothes for school?"

Hannah shook her head. "I'm saving for a pony. Ethan promised to help me pick one out."

Caroline bit back a sharp reply. Ethan knew no more about ponies than she did. Besides, encouraging the girl was cruel. Even if Hannah could save enough to buy one, which was highly unlikely, her next foster family might not have space for a pony.

Dreams, however, had their place, she reminded herself. They brought comfort and something to look forward to. Maybe Hannah's dreaming of a pony couldn't hurt, although the chances of her dream coming true were slim to none.

A horn sounded on the road and Ethan drove up in his pickup in a cloud of red dust.

She checked her watch and called to him through the open truck window. "Hi. Is it that late already?"

"You said three o'clock," Ethan said with a warm grin that threw off her equilibrium. "Hi, ladybug," he called to Hannah. "How's my favorite girl?"

"Hi, Ethan. I ate a blackberry."

"Only one?"

Hannah nodded.

Ethan climbed from the truck and grabbed a handful of berries from Caroline's pail. "They're like potato chips. You can't eat just one."

He popped the berries into his mouth, chewed, and swallowed. "Mmm-mmm. They taste almost as sweet as kisses."

"Chocolate kisses?" Hannah asked.

Ethan looked at Caroline. "Right. Chocolate kisses. They're the best kind. Until you're older."

Hannah looked from Ethan to Caroline as if

aware he was talking in a code she didn't understand.

The memory of kissing Ethan weakened Caroline's knees and her resolve to keep her distance. She groped for a change of subject to something safe. "How's your new sculpture coming?"

"It's almost finished. I'll show it to you when you pick up Hannah."

"I'd like that." Caroline gathered up the pails and cooler. "I have to go, sweetie. You'll be staying with Ethan for a little while, remember?"

"Okay."

"You can help me paint," Ethan said, "while Caroline visits her mother."

"I'd rather be painting, too," Caroline said with a grimace, "and you know how I feel about painting."

Ethan opened the passenger door of his truck and boosted Hannah onto the seat. He closed the door and turned to Caroline.

"Be glad you have a mother," he said in a voice too low for Hannah to hear.

"You're right." Caroline felt a pang of remorse, thinking of Hannah, who still cried herself to sleep at night, missing her mommy. "I'll keep that in mind."

"Say hello to Agnes for me." Ethan brushed Caroline's lips with a brief kiss and climbed into the truck. "We'll see you at supper."

He backed the truck into the drive, then turned it toward Orchard Cottage.

Caroline lifted her fingers to her lips. Black-berries were sweet, but nothing could match Ethan's kisses that, unfortunately, always left her feeling disoriented. She remained determined to leave the valley and have that ranch she'd always wanted, she reminded herself. Besides, the man had problems, secrets and a yen to return to Baltimore next summer. Even if she were looking for a permanent relationship—which she wasn't—she knew better than to follow a dead end.

Why did life have to be so complicated?

With a sigh, she walked toward the house to clean up before heading into town.

On the front porch of Orchard Cottage, Ethan handed Hannah an old but clean white T-shirt to pull over her new shorts and shirt. He glanced at the child's new sneakers. "Better take those off, so they don't get ruined."

Hannah sat cross-legged on the floor, ripped open the Velcro fastenings, and removed her tennis shoes. "What about my socks?"

"Those, too, or they'll get covered with paint."

"What are we painting?"

"My living room."

"What color?"

"Yellow. It reminds me of sunshine."

"Me, too," Hannah said, "but I don't know how to paint."

"It's easy. I'll show you. Or you could just watch, if you like."

Hannah shook her head. "I should help. It's only fair."

"How come?" The way the girl's mind worked fascinated him.

"Because you painted my room," she said in her solemn way.

"One good turn deserves another?"

She nodded.

"Who taught you that?"

"My mommy."

"You miss her, don't you, kid?"

Hannah nodded.

"My brother Jerry died a few months ago." He surprised himself with the admission.

"Do you still miss him?"

"I'll always miss him."

"But he lives in your heart, just like Mommy lives in my heart."

"Who told you that?" Ethan asked.

"Mr. Gofer, Daniel's friend."

Ethan felt the pain that had been his constant companion since Jerry's death ease the slightest fraction. "Mr. Gofer is a very wise man."

"That's what Daniel says."

"And your brother is a fine young man."

"I know." Hannah scrambled to her bare feet. "I'm ready to paint."

The kid was a wonder, better than antidepressants

or therapy. If she could survive what life had thrown at her, Ethan could, too. After less than three weeks in Pleasant Valley, with the help of Caroline and Hannah, he felt himself coming alive again. He was sleeping better at night, his anxieties had eased, and he found himself more often looking forward with eager anticipation instead of always backward with regret.

He opened the screen door and Hannah preceded him inside. He'd already placed drop cloths to protect the floors, so he poured sunny yellow paint called Lemon Chiffon into a tray and showed Hannah how to fill her roller.

With her tongue tucked in the corner of her mouth in concentration, Hannah began rolling color on the wall. Ethan grabbed a brush and started cutting in around the woodwork.

"So, how do you like living with Caroline?" he asked.

"She's nice. She smells good."

Wisteria. He could almost smell it himself, in spite of the paint fumes.

"And she's fun," Hannah added.

"How is she fun?"

"We read books. And watch movies and TV. Mostly about cowboys. Caroline really likes cowboys."

Ethan could have done without the reminder of Caroline's intended move.

"You shoulda been a cowboy," Hannah said.

"Me? Why?"

"Then you could marry Caroline."

Ethan stopped, his brush suspended, dripping paint. "What makes you say that?"

"I can tell you like her. And she likes you. But she wants to marry a cowboy."

"She told you that?"

Hannah stopped rolling paint and nodded. "She said if she ever gets married, it will be to a man who can help her run her ranch that she wants to own someday."

"When did she say that?"

"Last night, after we watched *Bonanza*. She said she'd like to live out west someday and have a ranch like the Ponderosa."

With a sinking sensation, Ethan returned to his painting. So much for his hope that he'd been making headway in winning Caroline's heart. According to Hannah, Caroline still had her sights set on her Western dream—and a cowboy to ride off into the sunset with. He would have sworn she'd responded to his kiss, but apparently not enough. Maybe she saw him merely as a diversion while she cooled her heels in the valley, waiting for Daniel to graduate and Hannah to get a new family.

He shook off feelings of self-pity. He had a year left to plead his case. The tranquility of Orchard Cottage was gradually healing his wounded psyche. He'd been able to talk about Jerry to

Hannah without coming apart at the seams. Who knew what other miracles might happen in the next twelve months?

Glad to escape her mother's complaints and accusations of abandonment, Caroline climbed the steps of Orchard Cottage. The blare of Asheville's country music radio station came from the living room when she knocked on the screen door.

"C'mon in," Ethan called above the country music. "We're taking a break. You're early."

"I didn't stay as long as I'd planned. Mama wasn't feeling well."

In fact, Agnes had clutched her chest and complained about her heart in a pathetic attempt to convince Caroline to return to live at the bed-and-breakfast. Agnes had improved remarkably, however, when Caroline had suggested her mother should move into an assisted care facility since her health was so bad. The visit had left Caroline feeling cranky and emotionally exhausted.

She stepped into the living room, empty except for the tarps on the floor and a portable radio, and felt immediately better. The walls glowed with a fresh, cheerful yellow, accented by beams of sunlight from the western windows. Ethan and Hannah sat cross-legged on the floor in a corner, drinking Cokes and eating Fritos and Ding Dongs.

Caroline started to protest about spoiling the child's supper, but Hannah looked so content, she didn't have the heart to ruin the child's good mood.

Hannah's hair, beautifully styled by Amy Lou two weeks ago into a close-cropped Peter Pan cut, was streaked with paint. The soles of her feet were yellow, and her thin little body was swathed in a huge T-shirt, also spattered with yellow. With her face smeared with paint and her mouth covered with Ding Dong icing, she appeared perfectly happy.

"Hi, Caroline. I helped Ethan paint."

"So I see. And you did a fine job."

"How's your mama?" Ethan asked.

Remembering her mother's complaints, Caroline suppressed a grimace. "Not great, but she's slowly coming around. Maybe by the time I move, she'll be used to the idea."

"You're moving?" Hannah eyes rounded with alarm. "What about me?"

Caroline could have smacked herself for her insensitive blunder. "I won't be moving for a long time, sweetie. You and I are staying put at Blackberry Farm until Daniel graduates a year from now."

She expected Hannah to ask what would happen after that, but a year was a lifetime for a little girl, and Caroline's answer erased the panic from the child's eyes. She took another bite of a Ding Dong.

"There's a clean towel and washcloth in the

bathroom," Ethan told Hannah. "The paint will come off with plenty of soap and water. How about cleaning up before getting in Caroline's car?"

He helped Hannah tug off the paint-stained shirt, and she skipped barefoot into the kitchen toward the bathroom.

Caroline glanced around the newly painted room, studying her surroundings to keep from looking at him. Why did the sight of him have to turn her knees to Jell-O? "You're making progress."

At least her voice didn't give away the emotional turmoil Ethan created in her. She sounded cool and collected—but then he couldn't see her palms sweating.

"On the cottage and my artwork, too. Want to see my newest work?"

"Sure." She was curious about the artistic abilities of a man who'd earned his living in the macho profession of firefighting. Following him through the kitchen, she called to Hannah in the bathroom, "We'll be in the barn, sweetie. Come on out with us when you've finished."

"Yes, ma'am," Hannah answered.

"Put on your shoes first," Ethan added. "I don't want you getting metal slivers in your feet."

"Okay."

"Want a Coke or some Fritos?" he asked Caroline. "I'm afraid we've polished off the Ding Dongs."

She shook her head. "No, thanks."

He held open the screen door, and she brushed past him as she crossed the threshold. To avoid temptation, she hurried down the stairs to the yard, but Ethan fell in step beside her. His presence was both comforting and disturbing.

"I've been meaning to ask," he said, "have you had a chance to look at Eileen's journals?"

"I've started reading them at night after Hannah's gone to sleep."

"And?" He adjusted his long-legged stride to match hers.

"The journals begin when Eileen came to Blackberry Farm as a bride. I've skimmed through the first six months, and she sounded deliriously happy, but I felt like an intruder. The journals obviously weren't meant to be shared."

"If she'd been concerned about her privacy, she would have burned them or instructed Rand to destroy them, wouldn't she?"

Caroline shrugged. "Maybe. If she'd thought about it."

"Any clues in her writings to the identity of the mystery body?"

"Nothing. In fact, now that you mention it, Eileen doesn't mention anyone coming to the farm. Just her and Calvin."

"They were honeymooners. They'd want to be alone." She could see his smile out of the corner of her eye.

Caroline nodded. "In her entries, Eileen wrote often about how much she loved him. And she said that Calvin liked seclusion. He insisted he wanted to keep her all to himself."

"I know what he meant," Ethan said.

Caroline stopped and stared at him. "You do?"

His hazel eyes, filled with promises, locked with hers, but his words contradicted the promise in his gaze. "I know how he felt about seclusion. I like it, too. It's good for my work."

Feeling off balance and disoriented, which was becoming her natural state around Ethan, she followed him into the cool dimness of the barn. In the center of the packed-earth floor, a tarp covered an object more than ten feet high and about the circumference of a child's wading pool.

"Let me turn on the lights." Ethan plugged in an extension to a spotlight, hung on a rafter, that centered on the tarp. Then, with a flick of his wrist, he jerked off the covering. "Well, what do you think?"

Caroline was speechless. Tortured columns of steel and rebar reached toward the ceiling of the barn like twisted skeletal fingers. Barbed wire and scraps of polished metal as honed as sharpened blades twined among the girders, a tangible representation of devastation, destruction and pain. She could almost hear the metal screaming.

"It's very powerful," she finally managed to say. "Almost overwhelming."

He nodded with grim satisfaction, apparently pleased by her assessment. "It isn't supposed to be pretty."

The image gripped her, like a train wreck. She wanted to look away but couldn't. "What does it represent?"

He gazed at the sculpture, his expression a strange mixture of pride and revulsion. "It represents the past. My past."

Caroline wanted to ask more, to inquire what horrible experience had precipitated the work before her, but Hannah skipped into the barn.

"I'm ready to go," the girl said.

Not wanting to discuss the origin of Ethan's sculpture in front of Hannah, who'd had enough trauma in her own life, Caroline took the child's hand.

"Okay, sweetie, let's go. We'll see you at supper, Ethan."

"I'll be there as soon as I've cleaned up. And thanks for your help, ladybug."

After supper, when Ethan had returned to his place and Hannah was asleep, Caroline couldn't get Ethan's disturbing artwork out of her mind. What horrible experience had caused him to create such a frightening image?

Unable to sleep and hoping to banish thoughts of Ethan, she grabbed a stack of Eileen's journals and curled into a corner of the parlor sofa to read. Picking up where she'd left off the night before, she skimmed through a few more months of Eileen's newlywed bliss. She was almost ready to stop reading and go to bed when the next entry brought her wide awake.

> Tonight Calvin hit me. I'd scorched the front of his favorite shirt with the iron, and when he saw it, he slapped me so hard, I fell to the floor. He was immediately repentant and gathered me up in his arms and cried, claiming he'd had a bad day, begging me to forgive him, and swearing it would never happen again. I've never seen that side of him before, and it frightens me.

Caroline skimmed ahead a few months and shuddered to read of Calvin's continued abuse and his attempts to convince Eileen that she deserved his ill treatment. Caroline picked up a later journal and found the entry made the day Calvin left for the war.

> Other wives are crying and despondent, but I feel only relief. The man who walked out that door was not the sweet, considerate man I married. He's become an unpredictable monster who can turn on me out of the blue, without warning. If I had

family or close friends to turn to, I would have run away by now, but I have no family and Calvin hasn't allowed me to become friends with anyone in the valley. Nor have I any money of my own. As a result, I have nowhere to go. People in the valley wouldn't believe me if I told them how he beats me. To the neighbors, Calvin is a model citizen. I hate to admit it, but I'm grateful for this war. If he hadn't gone away, I fear he would have killed me. Now, at least, I have time to contemplate what to do, how to escape before he returns.

Sickened by what she'd read, Caroline put down the journal, went to the secretary, and rummaged through the notebooks on the shelf until she found the notebook dated 1945. She wanted to know how Eileen had reacted to Calvin's death as a hero.

She opened the 1945 journal and began to read. During the war, Eileen had started picking blackberries and making jelly. She was saving the money from her jelly sales to fund her escape from the valley. Caroline grimaced at the irony. She'd discussed escaping the valley herself many times with Eileen, never knowing of Eileen's earlier escape plan.

Caroline turned the pages and continued

reading. Words jumped out at her from the page and took her breath away. She dropped the book and ran to the phone. With shaking fingers, she dialed Ethan's cell phone.

"Hello?" His voice was groggy.

She'd wakened him. Glancing at the clock on the mantel, she realized it was almost two o'clock.

"Caroline? Is everything okay?"

"No . . . I . . . ." Her voice shook as hard as her body. "I can't tell you on the phone."

"Hold on." His tone was firm, steady and reassuring. "I'll be right there."

Chapter Thirteen

Ethan sat at the kitchen table, his solid presence reassuring, his big hands curled around a mug of coffee. He hadn't uttered a word of complaint about being yanked from his bed by a call in the wee hours of the morning. Caroline had made coffee as soon as she'd hung up from summoning him, and she was grateful for his speedy arrival. It was going to be a long night, what little was left of it.

She filled a mug for herself and sat across from him at the table. Outside, katydids chattered in the woods and moonlight streamed across the lawn. All seemed peaceful and serene, unlike the horrible scenario she'd uncovered in Eileen's journals.

"I can't believe it." For one terrible instant, she feared she was going to cry and be unable to continue, but a gulp of scalding coffee doused the tears and steadied her.

"You'd better start at the beginning," Ethan said with appealing gentleness, "and tell me what's wrong. Is it Hannah? Your mother?"

She shook her head. "Mama's fine, and Hannah's out like a light after a day of berry picking and painting. It's Eileen."

His eyebrows lifted in surprise. "Eileen? You haven't been seeing ghosts?"

"In a manner of speaking." What she'd read would haunt her the rest of her days. "After you left tonight, I returned to reading Eileen's journals."

"More wedded bliss?" His expression turned dubious. "That can't be what has you so upset."

She couldn't beat around the bush. She had to tackle the horrible truth head on. "Eileen wrote more about how happy she was. Then things turned ugly fast."

"Ugly?"

"Calvin was an abuser. He began by hitting Eileen occasionally, then immediately begging her forgiveness. But the abuse worsened and became more frequent. Eileen was a beautiful woman, and Calvin was insanely jealous. He kept her a prisoner at Blackberry Farm. The only time she went to town, to church or to shop, he always accompanied her, and usually beat her when they returned, accusing her of making eyes at the men they encountered."

Ethan's face turned dark, like a thunderstorm about to break. "He sounds like a monster."

Caroline clasped her mug to warm the ice from her fingers. "It gets even worse."

Ethan reached across the table and took her hand. His flesh was warm and comforting, and she held on tight. A lump formed in her throat, making speech difficult.

"You don't have to tell me if it's too upsetting," he said. "I can read the journals myself, if you'd rather."

She shook her head. "Telling is quicker, and I need your help in deciding what to do."

"Okay." He gave her fingers a solacing squeeze. "I'm listening."

She sipped coffee and swallowed against the tightness in her throat. "When Calvin's abuse escalated, poor Eileen was trapped. She had no job skills, no money of her own, no family to turn to, and her husband had kept her isolated from the people in the valley, so she didn't even have a close friend to confide in. I'm guessing that writing in her journals was the only thing that kept her sane."

"Good thing Calvin didn't find them," Ethan said.

Caroline paled at the thought of what might have happened if he had.

"So she just gritted her teeth and took what he dished out?" The disgust in Ethan's voice reflected the frustration Caroline had felt ever since reading of Eileen's plight.

"She hung on until Calvin left for the war. Then she hoarded sugar rations and started making jelly. For the four years he was gone, she squirreled away her jelly money, saving it for her escape. She planned to flee Blackberry Farm before he returned."

"It's a good thing he never did," Ethan said with feeling.

"He did. He did come home."

Ethan scowled, his face scrunched in puzzlement. "Didn't you tell me earlier that he was killed in action and buried overseas?"

"That's what Eileen told everyone." Caroline took a deep breath and let it out slowly. "But she lied."

"What? Calvin didn't die?"

"He died, all right. Just not overseas."

"What happened?"

Caroline shivered, as if vibrations of the horror of the past still reverberated in the room. "According to her journal, Eileen received a telegram that Calvin had been wounded in action. Shortly afterward, the Japanese surrendered, and Eileen knew that as soon as Calvin had recovered, he'd return to Blackberry Farm. She began packing to leave—but she was too late. The night before she planned to disappear, Calvin returned. He hadn't let her know because he wanted to surprise her."

Ethan grimaced. "Some surprise."

Caroline nodded. "Actually, he told her he had wanted to appear unannounced so he could check up on her. His letters throughout the war had been filled with dire warnings of what would happen to her if she even so much as looked at another man."

"She didn't, did she?"

"No, but unfortunately, Calvin observed Joe Mauney leaving Blackberry Farm as he arrived—"

"—and jumped to the wrong conclusion?"

"Joe had been here to check on Eileen's sick cow. When Calvin came in and accused her of having an affair with Joe, she tried to explain, but her attempts only made him hit her harder. She was afraid for her life."

"So much for being a war hero," Ethan growled between clenched teeth.

"Unable to see out of one eye and with her shoulder dislocated by Calvin's attack, Eileen knew she was going to die. He told her he wasn't afraid of killing, that it was all he'd done for the past few years. He sat at this very table and demanded that she fix him a meal first. He promised he'd make her pay for her infidelity afterward."

Still clutching her hand, Ethan said, "The chat

room where I met Eileen was for people with post-traumatic stress disorder. Eileen never told us about the trauma in her life. Now I understand."

Caroline wanted to ask what trauma Ethan had suffered, but she needed to finish Eileen's story first. "It gets worse."

"Did she run away?"

"She couldn't. Calvin wouldn't let her out of his sight. Knowing that she wouldn't live through the night, Eileen grabbed a heavy iron skillet under the pretense of cooking supper. When Calvin sat at the table, with her one good arm, she swung the skillet with all her strength and hit him in the back of the head, crushing his skull. He died instantly."

Comprehension registered on Ethan's face. "Calvin Bickerstaff is the unidentified body I found at Orchard Cottage."

Caroline nodded. "Eileen knew she couldn't call the police. No one in the valley had known of Calvin's abuse, and she feared no one would believe that she'd acted in self-defense. In addition, Calvin had already been written up in the local paper as a war hero. The odds of a jury letting Eileen off for killing him weren't good."

"But her shoulder was dislocated," Ethan said. "How did she get such a big man out of here and up to the cottage?"

"Desperation gave her strength. She reset her own shoulder—"

Ethan winced, apparently familiar with that painful procedure.

"And once she'd recovered from the beating Calvin had given her, she dragged the body out to her car and drove him to the cottage, which had stood empty since the beginning of the war. She dug a shallow grave beside the barn. That was all she could manage in her weakened state, according to her journal."

Ethan nodded. "That red clay is hard as rock."

"To make certain the body wasn't uncovered by wild animals, she moved an existing compost pile from the back of the barn one shovelful at a time to anchor the grave. Several days later, she called the local newspaper and told them the military had advised her that Calvin had died of his wounds and been buried in Hawaii."

"And nobody raised questions?"

"Not a one. Like Eileen, Calvin had no family and no friends. With so many men dying, his passing was just another in a long list of war fatalities."

Ethan shook his head in amazement. "And she kept her secret for all those years."

"It would have gone to her grave with her, if not for her journals."

Ethan still held her hand, his fingers interlaced with hers. He gave her a gentle squeeze, and his eyes, deep brown flecked with green, filled with understanding, as if he had guessed Caroline's dilemma. "So, will you tell Lucas about Calvin?"

"To tell would betray Eileen's memory. I don't want folks in the valley thinking of her as a murderer. She was a good, kind woman who never hurt a soul and helped a lot of people."

Ethan appeared thoughtful. "It isn't as if Calvin has family somewhere wondering what happened to him."

"But I'd have to lie to the police." Caroline shuddered. "My mama raised me to tell the truth and respect the law. I know I should keep Eileen's secret, but not telling doesn't feel right, either."

Ethan stood, rounded the table and pulled her to her feet. Encircling her with his arms, he gazed into her eyes. "That's just one of reasons I love you."

His admission took her breath away. He'd kissed her, but he'd never said he loved her.

"What?" she stammered.

"Calvin Bickerstaff didn't know what love meant," Ethan said. "He should have cherished Eileen, kept her safe, made her happy." His expression and tone softened. "That's what I want to do for you, Caroline, if you'll let me."

Part of her wanted nothing more than to melt into his arms and give in to his promises. But her practical side held back, reminding her how little she knew of Ethan and his tortured past. He must have read the conflict in her expression.

"You don't have to decide now," he said. "We have a year, and I'm a very patient man."

Her thoughts spun in confusion. "I . . . don't know what to say."

Hope gleamed in his eyes. "Don't say anything. We have plenty of time."

And with that, Ethan leaned down and kissed her until all thoughts of tortured pasts had fled from her mind, leaving only love.

Chapter Fourteen

For the umpteenth time in three days, Caroline felt like banging her head against the wall. She'd promised herself not to get involved and yet she couldn't stop thinking of Ethan's declaration of love. She tried to rationalize that learning of Eileen's horrible experience had knocked her off-kilter emotionally, which was why she'd let him kiss her. But she knew that excuse was a lie. She'd *wanted* to kiss Ethan, plain and simple.

Well, maybe not so simple. She'd hoped that kiss would clear him from her system. But the result had been the exact opposite. She couldn't get him out of her mind. He'd said he'd loved her, a statement that had taken her breath—and her capacity for rational thought—away. And the fact that Ethan hadn't shown up at the house since hadn't helped her regain her equilibrium. Several times a day, he drove by in his truck without slowing or stopping, so Caroline knew he was okay. But why was he avoiding her? Did he regret his declaration of love?

The man had her spinning in circles, not knowing which side was up and unable to do a single thing to set herself straight again. All she could think of was Ethan and the sound of his voice telling her how much he loved her.

She missed him.

And if she missed him now, after only three days without seeing him, how would she survive when she moved to New Mexico? What in heaven had she gone and done?

If it weren't for Hannah, Caroline feared she would have lost her mind entirely. Only keeping busy kept her sane. Working together in the kitchen, they had made enough jelly to stock the roadside stand, and for the past two days, sales had been brisk along Valley Road. Last night, Hannah had counted the profits and put them aside in her pony fund. Although Caroline had assured the girl it might take years to raise the money for a pony, Hannah had insisted she'd keep saving until she had enough.

In the late afternoon of the third day of Ethan's mysterious avoidance, Caroline and Hannah had closed and locked the shutters on the stand, taken the cash box, and were walking up the drive toward the farm.

"That Mr. Trace sure bought a lot of jelly," Hannah said. "A whole boxful of jars. He almost doubled my pony fund."

"He has a lot of boys to feed at Archer Farm," Caroline said. "And now Daniel will be enjoying the jelly you made. How about that?"

"I'm glad. Daniel's a good brother."

"He's an excellent brother. You're very lucky to have him."

"Do you have any brothers?"

Caroline shook her head.

"Sisters?"

"No, just me."

"But you have a mommy." Hannah's tone was wistful. "Will I ever have a new mommy?"

The sound of a horn on the road behind them saved Caroline from answering. She turned to see Ethan's truck approaching, pulling a trailer.

A horse trailer.

Caroline's pulse raced, her mouth went dry, and she expected Ethan to drive by as he'd done the past three days. He surprised her by stopping beside them and hopping out of the cab. His face glowed with excitement, like a kid's at Christmas. Just seeing him kick-started Caroline's heartbeat to a gallop, reminding her how much she'd wanted to see him.

"Hey, good-looking ladies," he said with a grin. "Glad I ran into you. I have a special delivery for Hannah."

"For me?" Hannah said. "What is it?"

Ethan couldn't have looked more pleased with himself if he'd won the lottery. "You'll see in a minute. But first, I want both of you to close your eyes."

Caroline, hoping her guess was wrong and that he'd borrowed a horse trailer to haul supplies, shot him a warning glance. Beside her, Hannah squeezed her eyes shut.

"No fair peeking," Ethan warned, and Caroline closed her eyes.

She heard his footsteps on the gravel as he walked to the rear of the trailer. She noted the metallic squeal of the hinges as a door opened and flinched at the bump of a lowering ramp. Next came the unmistakable clop of hooves and a soft whinny. She opened her eyes to watch him lead a tiny Shetland pony around the back of the trailer toward Hannah.

"You've got to be kidding," she said.

Ethan shook his head. "Open your eyes, Hannah."

Hannah took one look at the pony, and her jaw dropped. "Is it really for me?"

"All yours, ladybug," Ethan said. "Special delivery all the way from Georgia."

"A pony for me?" Hannah repeated breathlessly. "Oh, thank you, Ethan."

"You're welcome," he said.

"You bought a horse in Georgia?" Caroline was flabbergasted.

"Not a horse, a pony. And I didn't buy it. Grant Nathan helped me rescue it through the ASPCA."

Hannah, oblivious to their conversation, had

thrown one arm around the pony's neck and was stroking its muzzle.

"Rescued?" Caroline knew Grant had been active in dog rescues, but she hadn't realized people also rescued horses.

"The previous owners abandoned it," Ethan explained. "If it hadn't found a new home," he lowered his voice to a whisper, "it would have been put down."

She didn't know whether to smack him or kiss him. A pony fulfilled Hannah's wildest dream, but . . . "We know nothing about taking care of a pony."

"Not to worry," Ethan promised breezily. "Grant sent along everything you'll need, including books. They're in my truck."

In spite of her exasperation, Caroline couldn't help smiling. "Like a car's owner's manual? I can never make heads nor tails of those."

"Identifying the head and tail is the easy part," Ethan said, so reasonably she wanted to grind her teeth. "And Grant said to call him or Dr. Stratton if you have any questions or problems. No charge for Miss Hannah. And I'll clean out a stall in your barn to make a place for it, as soon as I return Grant's trailer."

Caroline wanted to tell him to take the pony back, that she didn't need the complication of an animal to care for, but seeing the adoration and contentment on Hannah's face froze the words in her throat. Reluctantly accepting that she now had a pony as well as a foster daughter, Caroline sighed. "We can't keep calling it *it*. The pony needs a name."

"That's Hannah's department. Your pony needs a name, ladybug. What do you want to call it?"

Hannah gazed deep into the pony's eyes, rimmed with lighter hair that made it appear to be wearing glasses. She thought for a moment, then looked back to Ethan and Caroline.

"Well," Caroline said with gentle encouragement. "Do you have an idea for a name?"

Hannah nodded solemnly.

"Want to share?" Ethan prodded.

Hannah's grave expression lifted in a dazzling smile, and, miracle of miracles, she giggled. "Can I really name him anything I want?"

"Anything," Caroline promised, especially if it made the child laugh.

"Then I want to call him Harry Trotter."

Ethan and Caroline burst out laughing at the play on words, and Hannah joined in.

"I can't believe it," the girl said. "It's like magic. My very own pony. Thank you, Ethan."

"You can thank me best," he said, "by taking very good care of Harry, so he doesn't cause extra work for Caroline."

"I promise." Hannah, obviously in love, flung her arms around the pony's neck. "Can I ride him?"

"Not yet," Caroline said. "You should get better acquainted first. Why don't you walk him into the pasture and see if he wants some grass?" She looked to Ethan. "Ponies do eat grass, don't they?"

"Some rancher you'll make. You don't even know what horses eat. Just think of Harry as a starter kit."

Hannah took Harry's lead and led him through a break in the split-rail fence into the meadow, leaving Caroline and Ethan standing on the drive. Alone together for the first time since he'd said he loved her, she felt tongue-tied and awkward. She didn't know what to say. How could she, when she hadn't sorted out her feelings about the man who was constantly surprising her, first with his declaration of love, then a three-day disappearance, and now this incredibly thoughtful gift for Hannah. No wonder she stayed off balance in his presence.

"What will happen to Harry when I leave the valley next year and Hannah has to move?" she asked.

"If Hannah's new foster family can't keep him, Grant promised to find the pony a home where Hannah can visit, possibly at Archer Farm."

Her frustration erupted as anger. "You've thought of everything, haven't you?"

He leaned forward and kissed her gently on the lips. "Not everything. I'm still working on how to keep you from moving west."

Before she could reply, he sprinted back to his truck and climbed inside.

"I have to return Grant's trailer," he called through the open window, "then prepare Harry's stall. See you at supper."

With her hands on her hips, she watched him continue up the road and turn around at the farmhouse. He passed her again, blew her a kiss and disappeared in a cloud of dust on his way to the highway.

With a shake of her head, she turned and headed toward the meadow to join Hannah and Harry, wondering what complication life would throw at her next.

Ethan whistled while he worked, glad for the gusty breeze that cooled the interior of the barn. The air smelled of ozone and approaching rain, and he hurried to complete his last weld before the late August storm hit. His latest sculpture, a tangible manifestation of how far he'd come in healing, was almost finished. The stylistic representation of a little girl on a galloping pony, her hair blowing in the wind, was upbeat and positive, a far cry from the pessimism and pain captured in his earlier piece.

Two months at Orchard Cottage had made the difference. Gofer had recommended routine and security for Hannah. The same prescription had worked for Ethan. Remodeling the cottage and creating his sculptures had filled his days, and Caroline and Hannah had filled his evenings and weekends. Together they'd explored the town and surrounding countryside. He'd abandoned the isolation he'd sought for so long. With Caroline, he'd visited Rand and Brynn, Merrilee and Grant, and Jodie and Jeff. Archer Farm had become like a second home, since he and Caroline took Hannah there often to visit Daniel.

The one thing he hadn't done was what he wanted most of all—kiss Caroline again. But he'd decided not to push her. In spite of the time they'd spent together, she still talked about leaving the valley next summer. If Caroline loved him and wanted a life with him, she'd have to make the first move. He loved her enough to live wherever she wanted, but he knew winning her heart was more complicated than simply finding a place to call home. She'd stated clearly that she wanted her independence, and he'd do nothing to make her feel tied to him or the valley. If she loved him enough to commit, she'd have to come to him of her own free will, make her own choices and not feel that he'd backed her into a corner where she didn't want to be. He still had ten months to persuade her. And he'd learned that the best persuasion was merely being there, no strings attached.

The barn had darkened from the gathering clouds, and he hurried to put away his equipment before the rains came. He was dashing to the back porch as the first fat drops of water fell. He paused before entering the house and glanced toward Blackberry Farm. A bolt of lightning split the sky with a concurrent crash of thunder. The streak speared the roof of Caroline's barn and hung there, seemingly forever, its glare so bright, it hurt his eyes.

Ethan blinked. And when his vision cleared from the brilliance, through the sheet of rain, he could see the plume of smoke and lick of flames curling from the barn roof.

He bolted from the porch, tugged his cell phone from his pocket and punched in 911 as he raced for his truck.

Chapter Fifteen

Caroline struggled to breathe in the thick, moist air and glanced up the highway toward the west. A storm was coming. Thunderheads were building over the mountains and heading her way. Hannah perched on a stool inside the stand, reading a book while waiting for customers.

"Better run on home before the storm hits, sweetie. I'll close the stand. Is Harry in his stall?"

"Yes, ma'am." Hannah closed her book and slid from the stool. "I promised him we'd go riding this afternoon."

"You'll have to wait till the storm passes. Hurry, now, so you don't get wet."

Obedient as always, Hannah skipped up the drive toward the house. Caroline watched her go with a sweet ache beneath her breastbone. In a matter of only a few weeks, the little girl had managed to put a lock on her heart so strong that Caroline couldn't remember how life had been without her.

She roused from her contemplation and assessed the oncoming storm. If she hurried, she could make the house before the weather broke. One by one, she released the braces that held up the shutters of the stand, lowered them, and latched them in place. She picked up the cash box and locked the door with its padlock before starting up the drive. The storm was moving faster than she'd estimated, and windblown rain stung her face. She was glad Hannah had had time to make it to the house before the torrent started.

A tremendous clash of thunder almost deafened her, and as she peered through the rain, lightning struck the roof of the barn, hanging in the air, skewering the building with intense heat and light for several horrifying seconds. Sheets of water washed over her, almost obscuring her view, but not enough to hide the flames erupting from the shingles where the lightning had hit.

The barn was on fire.

And Harry was inside.

Her heart lodged in her throat. *Please, don't let Hannah go after him.*

Caroline ran, but the wind and rain beat against her, slowing her down. She stumbled and almost fell, but sheer panic kept her going. Her wet sneakers lost traction on the porch steps, and she slid and banged her knee. But the intense pain was insignificant compared to her concern for Hannah.

"Hannah! Where are you?" The screen door slammed behind her, but Hannah didn't answer.

"Hannah!" Caroline screamed again and grabbed the handset from the phone in the hall before hurrying to the kitchen. By the time she reached the back porch, the barn was engulfed in flames and spewing smoke, in spite of the pelting rain.

And Hannah was running straight toward the barn door.

"Hannah, stop!"

The wind grabbed her words and flung them away. Hannah didn't break her stride and plunged into the inferno.

Caroline punched 911 into the phone. "Fire at Blackberry Farm," she told the operator. "Send help."

She flung the handset aside and headed for the blaze, just as Ethan's truck screeched to a stop in front of the barn and Ethan leaped from the cab.

"Hannah," Caroline shouted with a sob, "she's inside."

"Stay back," Ethan shouted. "I'll get her."

Stripping off his shirt as he ran, Ethan, too, disappeared into the smoke and flames.

Caroline tried to follow but the heat beat her back. She paced on the back lawn, oblivious to the soaking rain, her gaze locked on the doorway to hell into which the two most important people in her life had disappeared.

From inside the barn came Harry's screams of fear and the sound of hooves hammering the wall of his stall. Seconds dragged like hours, and with every beat of her rapid pulse, Caroline faced the likelihood that she might never see Hannah or Ethan alive again. She jumped as a rafter cracked, broke, and brought down a section of roof as it fell.

Please, she thought, *just let them be safe, and I'll get my priorities straight. I don't care about a ranch in New Mexico. All I want are Hannah and Ethan, alive and whole, to spend the rest of my life with.*

But the more time that passed, the less likely it seemed that anyone would survive the roaring blaze.

Then, through a swirl of smoke, she glimpsed a movement, a tall form silhouetted by the flames behind it. Ethan stepped out of the haze.

With Hannah in his arms, and Harry's lead in his hands, he strode from the burning building with Harry trotting behind. Ethan had covered the pony's eyes with his shirt.

"Ethan!" Caroline raced toward them.

"Take Hannah." His voice wheezed from smoke inhalation, and he thrust the girl into her arms. "I'll get Harry to a safe place."

Sirens sounded and fire engines rumbled up the gravel drive, light bars flashing. Within minutes, the yard was filled with trucks, hoses and firefighters.

Caroline, with Hannah in her arms, retreated to the porch, out of the way.

"Are you all right, sweetie?" She choked back a sob of relief.

Hannah's face was smeared with soot, and she couldn't stop coughing. Caroline checked her over carefully, but didn't find any burns. The child's clothes weren't even singed.

"You should never have gone in there. Didn't you hear me call you?"

Still coughing, Hannah shook her head. When she could finally catch enough breath to speak, she looked up with innocent eyes. "I couldn't leave Harry, could I? He would have died."

Caroline gathered the girl in her arms and hugged her tight. "You both would have died if it weren't for Ethan."

Hannah struggled to free herself from Caroline's embrace. "Where's Harry? Is he okay?"

Caroline peered through the pouring rain and pointed. "He's there. Tied to the far corner of the porch out of the way. He looks fine."

But where was Ethan?

The torrent of rain eased, and she spotted Ethan among the firefighters, his bare torso black with soot as he grappled a length of hose, his hair and jeans plastered to his skin by rain. She was overcome by a rush of love.

"Ethan's a hero," Hannah said with a sigh. "He saved Harry and me."

"Yes," Caroline said with conviction. "He certainly is."

Then her heart stopped as Ethan, fire hose in hand, walked back into the blazing barn.

Caroline couldn't watch. She had to trust that Ethan, a veteran firefighter, knew what he was doing. "Come with me, Hannah. Those men will need food once the fire's out. After a quick wash to get rid of that soot, you can help make sand-wiches."

Seeking reassurance that her pony was okay, Hannah cast a glance at Harry, contentedly munching grass beneath an apple tree, before following Caroline into the kitchen.

At the sound of a crash that shook the floor beneath them, they turned and stared out the screen door. The barn had collapsed from the flames.

Ethan! His name screamed in her heart, and she stumbled with grief until she recognized him, standing safely among the other firefighters at a distance from the collapsed structure.

"Oh, Caroline, your beautiful barn. It's ruined." Hannah's eyes teared with sadness.

Caroline released the breath she'd been holding. "Barns can be rebuilt, sweetie. I'm so grateful that you and Ethan and Harry are all right."

Hannah's sorrowful expression brightened. In an unexpected and totally uncharacteristic move, she threw her arms around Caroline and squeezed with all her might. "I love you, Caroline."

Overcome with affection and gratitude, Caroline hugged her back and struggled to find her voice. "I love you, too, sweetie."

The violent storm passed as quickly as it had approached. By the time the firefighters had finished mopping up hot spots, the sun had come out, casting prisms of light among the droplets of water glistening on the ruined timbers.

Ethan, grimy and soaked with water and sweat, sat on the porch steps with Josh Mauney, Joe's son, Tom Fulton from the department store, Jay-Jay from the garage and the other well-trained volunteers of the Pleasant Valley fire department. Caroline and Hannah moved among them, serving thick ham sandwiches and iced tea.

Ethan couldn't stop smiling. Not only had he saved Hannah and Harry, he'd conquered his demons. He'd been so concerned for Hannah that without hesitation, without the constriction in his chest or uncontrollable tremors in his hands, he'd rushed straight into the burning barn to do the job he was trained to do. And he'd done it well. Even though they hadn't saved the barn, they'd kept the blaze from spreading to the outbuildings and the house, and no one had been hurt. He was a little shaky now, as he always was when the adrenaline rush faded and he was running on its fumes, but for the first time since Jerry's death, he felt almost whole again. Caroline's words of gratitude and the warmth in her eyes spiked his good mood even higher. After a run of horrible luck, maybe fate was finally working in his favor.

He'd wanted to grab Caroline and hold her when he'd read the message of love in her eyes, but he had one more task to complete before asking her to spend her life with him. She didn't know the full story. Actually, *he* didn't know the full story. Maybe his demons were only hiding and would eventually return. He had to tell Caroline the whole truth and let her decide whether he was worth the risk.

As the firemen finished up their work, he slid into the cab of his truck and headed home. He wanted to talk to Caroline, but first he needed a good scrub and fresh clothes.

At the sound of a truck backing out of the yard, Caroline looked up from her conversation with Tom Fulton to see Ethan's truck pulling away. Her heart sank. She hadn't had a chance to thank him properly for rescuing Hannah and Harry, and he'd left without even a goodbye.

But what had she expected? He was a firefighter, after all, and had only done his job.

But he was more than that, her heart insisted, would always be so much more than just a fireman or an artist or the tenant who leased her cottage. Watching him rush into those flames had made her realize how much she loved him, how she'd come to count on his presence in her life, as necessary as air and sunshine.

She'd also realized where her heart belonged. Not in some distant, nonexistent ranch out west. Her fantasy was merely that—a fantasy, a dream as insubstantial as air. But Ethan and Hannah were solid, real, flesh and blood whom she loved better than her own life. And Blackberry Farm was all the home she'd ever need.

"What?" she realized she hadn't heard a word Tom had been saying.

"I said I hope insurance will build you a new barn." Tom smiled and his teeth flashed white in his grimy face. "We haven't had a good old-fashioned barn raising in the valley in a long time. One way or another, we'll get it rebuilt for you."

Josh Mauney stood beside him. "If you need a place for the pony in the meantime, you can bring it to our farm."

Emotion welled in her throat. These men and their fellow volunteers had risked their lives to save her property, and now they were offering even more help. She wondered if there was another place in the world where such goodness and generosity prevailed.

"Thank you all, for everything."

"That's why we're here, missy." Jay-Jay had coiled the last hose onto the truck. "Just doing our job. And your tenant knows his stuff." He surveyed the yard, looking for Ethan. "Didn't get a chance to thank him for his help."

The men climbed into their vehicles and rolled down the drive at a much slower pace than their arrival. Caroline reached for Hannah's hand. "C'mon, sweetie. A nice bubble bath will soak out the stench of all that smoke."

Two hours later, after a supper where Ethan hadn't appeared, Caroline tucked a sweet-smelling, well-fed, and exhausted Hannah into bed. Tonight when she planted a kiss on the girl's forehead, Hannah lifted her arms and hugged Caroline around the neck. In that instant, Hannah became her child, the daughter she would love and nurture and raise to adulthood. Even if she had to do it alone.

She tucked the sheet around Hannah, who was already half asleep, checked that the daisy night light was on, and left the room, closing the door behind her.

When she reached the foot of the stairs, she started at the unexpected sight of Ethan, standing in front of the fireplace in the parlor. Happiness flooded her—until she noted his somber expression.

"Are you all right?" she asked. "We missed you at supper."

"Took a little longer than I expected to get rid of the smoke and soot." Raw emotion edged his voice, and agony creased his face. "There's something I have to tell you."

She braced herself for the worst and hoped for the best. Gesturing to a chair on one side of the fireplace, she sat opposite it. "Sit down. I'm listening."

He folded his lanky frame into the chair and clasped his big, strong and gentle hands between his knees. "I killed my brother."

She jerked her head up with surprise, certain that she'd heard wrong. "I don't believe it."

He nodded and his eyes glistened with moisture. "It's true."

But she still didn't believe it, not for a minute. A man as kind, as loving, as compassionate as Ethan wasn't capable of murder. There had to be more to the story. "You'd better tell me everything."

Ethan caught her gaze and held it. "I've needed to talk about it, but I haven't been able to, not to anyone—until now."

"Why now?" Her voice cracked as she struggled to keep her feelings from spilling over.

The barest glimmer of a smile broke through the

sadness on his face. "Because of you, Hannah, this farm, this valley, and its people."

She nodded, not wanting to interrupt the flow of his story.

Ethan leaned back in his chair and wiped his hand over his forehead, as if wanting to erase the memories stored there. He took a deep breath, like a man preparing to plunge off a high dive, then released it. "It happened last February.

"We got a call at the firehouse around midnight. An abandoned warehouse in the waterfront district was ablaze. The cops feared homeless people who used it for shelter were trapped inside. We rolled the engines."

He shook his head. "Jerry, my brother, was all pumped up. He loved fighting fires even more than I did, and that was saying something. At first I'd been afraid he'd become a fireman just to imitate me, his big brother, but he was a natural, like it was in his blood."

He paused and Caroline waited, not knowing where his story was headed. The grandfather clock chimed in the hall, and outside the open window, a whip-poor-will called in the warm summer darkness.

"Jerry was good," Ethan said, "but he wasn't a hot dog. He was careful, played by the book. When we reached the scene, the supervisor sent us on search and rescue to locate the homeless and get them out while the others fought the fire."

In her mind's eye, Caroline could see him, decked out in his heavy gear, walking unafraid into the blaze, just as he'd run into the barn this afternoon.

"We did a grid search of the building," Ethan continued, "and found no one. We were turning to leave when I saw Jerry's face through his mask. I could tell by his eyes a split second before it happened that something was wrong."

Ethan squeezed his eyes shut, as if trying to block the sight in his memory.

Caroline waited a moment, then prompted gently, "What happened?"

Ethan opened his eyes and cleared his throat before he was able to continue. "The floor gave way beneath him. One minute he was standing in front of me. The next he was gone. I flung myself facedown and inched across the floor toward the hole where he'd disappeared. He was dangling from a floor joist by one hand. I reached for him, and he grabbed me with his free hand, then released the joist and gripped my other hand. The flames from the floor below were all around us, but I couldn't let go. I knew I had to hang on until help arrived to pull him out, because as hard as I tried, I couldn't get enough of a grip to pull him free."

He looked at her with a twisted grin. "You've heard that old song, 'He Ain't Heavy, He's My Brother'?"

She nodded and blinked away tears.

"He was my brother, but with all his equipment, he weighed a ton. I hung on with everything I had until I thought my arms would pull from their sockets. I knew the others would come for us. All I had to do was hold on long enough.

"Jerry screamed to let him go, to get out and save myself. Called me a stubborn bastard. I told him nothing he called me could compare to what Mom would say if I left him." He swallowed hard. "But Mom never said a word, except that she didn't blame me. That Jerry had died doing what he loved."

Caroline's heart broke for Ethan. "You couldn't hold him?"

Ethan shook his head. "My gloves slipped off. Jerry plunged straight through to the floor below." Ethan paused, as if fighting for breath, and a single tear spilled over and slid down the contour of his rugged cheek. "He was still holding my gloves when we found him."

The burns on his hands, Caroline thought. That explained them. "But *you* didn't kill him. You did everything you could to save him."

Ethan tapped his forehead. "Intellectually I know that." He placed his hand over his heart. "But here I'll always feel I failed him."

Caroline shook her head. "I didn't know Jerry, but I doubt very much that he'd want you beating yourself up over this."

"There's more you have to know."

She steeled herself for bad news. Maybe the barn fire had resurrected too many bad memories and Ethan was going to leave, to flee them and the valley as he'd fled Baltimore. "I'm still listening."

"I fell apart when Jerry died. Anxiety, depression, night terrors, nightmares. I couldn't work. My throat closed up at the slightest whiff of smoke and I couldn't breathe. I went to a therapist, took meds, but nothing seemed to help. That's when I joined the online chat room for people dealing with post-traumatic stress disorder. That's where I met Eileen."

"Calvin's murder must have haunted her for her entire life. I'm glad we decided to keep it our secret. She suffered enough in life. At least now she can rest in peace."

Ethan nodded. "I'll always be grateful for her offering me a place where I'd have peace and quiet and space to heal."

He caught her gaze and smiled, like the sun sliding from behind a cloud. "And I did heal. Every day I've been here in the valley with you, I've grown stronger. The nightmares have ended. And I was able to run into the burning barn for Hannah and Harry without hesitating. A month ago, I would have frozen, been unable to act."

Caroline recalled the sculpture of tortured metal in Ethan's barn. His past, he'd called it. Now it all made sense.

Ethan rose from his chair, knelt before her and gathered her hands in his. She looked at his horrible scars as badges of honor.

"I want to spend the rest of my life," he said, "here with you and Hannah. I want to marry you, Caroline, if you'll have me."

Her heart had been breaking with sadness. Now it flooded with joy. She started to answer, but he pressed his fingers against her lips.

"Don't answer yet. There's something else you must consider."

"What?"

"I don't know if I'm completely healed. The nightmares, the anxiety, the whole PTSD ball of wax could recur, hit me when I least expect it. That's a lot to ask anyone to share. You have to factor that in to any decision you make."

Caroline nodded, undeterred. "Eileen always said that life doesn't come with guarantees. That all we have is one day at a time. I can't think of anything I'd rather do than spend one day at a time with you, Ethan, for the rest of my life."

"You wouldn't rather wait for your cowboy?" he said, half teasing, half worried.

She flung her arms around him. "Ethan Garrison, I wouldn't trade you for all the cowboys in Texas."

Epilogue

The early June day was mild and bright, perfect weather for the outdoor event. Ethan gazed around the tables set up on the lawn, and his heart filled with happiness at the sight of his friends.

Merrilee and Grant pushed back from their chairs to chase Sophia, who'd toddled off in pursuit of a butterfly. Rand and Brynn smiled at Jared as Jodie placed her five-month-old baby in the little boy's outstretched arms, and Jeff beamed with pride at his son.

The boys and staff from Archer Farm stood in line for seconds at the buffet table on the front porch. Sitting at tables scattered across the lawn, neighbors and friends from town chatted in small groups over empty plates and refilled glasses of sweet iced tea. Even Agnes, sitting with Aunt Mona, seemed to be having a good time. Being on her own had been good for Agnes. She'd reconciled herself to Caroline's leaving home, and had become less clingy, and had surprised everyone by doting on Hannah and Daniel.

Ethan had found his peace in the valley. And with that peace had come love, contentment and a sense of accomplishment. Orchard Cottage and Meadow Place had been completely restored and rented. And Merrilee, through her contacts with

New York City art galleries, had enabled Ethan to sell his sculptures at prices that guaranteed he'd never have to work again.

But he was working. He'd joined the Pleasant Valley Fire and Rescue, who, fortunately, weren't called out often, giving him plenty of time not only to continue to restore the farm and create his art but to be a husband and father, too.

He glanced at Caroline, sitting beside him, and his heart swelled with love. It was time. He stuck two fingers in his mouth and gave a sharp whistle. At the sound, the guests gave him their attention.

"Thank you all for coming today," he began. "We have many things to celebrate and we appreciate your sharing in our happiness. First, I want to congratulate Daniel on his graduation from high school and his winning a scholarship to the University of South Carolina in Columbia."

Everyone clapped, and the Archer Farm contingent burst into loud cheers and whistles. At his place at the table beside Hannah and Caroline, Daniel blushed and pushed to his feet for a brief bow to acknowledge the approval.

"But that's not all the good news," Ethan continued. "We're also here today to celebrate Hannah and Daniel's official entry into our family. Their adoption has gone through the paperwork hoops and they are now legally what they've been in reality for almost a year, Hannah and Daniel Garrison, our daughter and son."

Cheers and applause rang out again, and Ethan waited for them to cease before he sprung the surprise he'd worked so hard to pull off. From his vantage point, he caught a glimpse of Grant, who had disappeared at the beginning of Ethan's announcements and now waited almost out of sight around a curve in the drive.

Ethan grabbed Caroline's hand and pulled her to her feet beside him. "Today," he announced, "is also the six-month anniversary of our wedding, and I have a little present for my wife."

Hearing his cue, Grant started up the drive, leading behind him two horses, complete with saddles and bridles.

He heard Caroline's swift intake of breath, saw the surprise and pleasure flash across her beloved face, and knew his gift was a hit.

"You always wanted a horse," he said. "I figured we'd learn to ride together. Who knows? Maybe I should have been a cowboy. We'll find out."

While their guests cheered, Caroline threw her arms around his neck, stood on tiptoe, and kissed him. "Cowboy or not, you're the best man on the planet, and I'm proud to be your wife."

"Enough of that mushy stuff," Hannah interrupted. "Let Daniel cut his cake."

Ethan slung his arm around Daniel's shoulder, and Caroline took Hannah by the hand. Together they climbed the porch steps to the buffet table where a huge sheet cake shaped like a mortar-board with tassel waited. Daniel cut the slices, Hannah held the plates, and Caroline scooped ice cream to serve their friends.

One big happy family.

Ethan felt moisture prick the back of his eyelids. Life was good and getting better every day. He was one lucky man.

CHARLOTTE DOUGLAS

The major passions of Charlotte Douglas's life are her husband—her high school sweetheart to whom she's been married for more than four decades—and writing compelling stories. A national bestselling author, she enjoys filling her books with love of home and family, special places and happy endings.

With their two cairn terriers, she and her husband live most of the year on Florida's central west coast, but spend the warmer months at their North Carolina mountaintop retreat.

Center Point Large Print
600 Brooks Road / PO Box 1
Thorndike, ME 04986-0001 USA

(207) 568-3717

US & Canada:
1 800 929-9108
www.centerpointlargeprint.com